My Father's Wives

Mike Greenberg

ωm

WILLIAM MORROW
An Imprint of HarperCollins*Publishers*

MY FATHER'S WIVES. Copyright © 2015 by Mike Greenberg. All rights reserved. Printed in the United States of America. No part of this book may be used or reproduced in any manner whatsoever without written permission except in the case of brief quotations embodied in critical articles and reviews. For information address HarperCollins Publishers, 195 Broadway, New York, NY 10007.

HarperCollins books may be purchased for educational, business, or sales promotional use. For information please e-mail the Special Markets Department at SPsales@harpercollins.com.

FIRST EDITION

Designed by Lisa Stokes

Library of Congress Cataloging-in-Publication Data has been applied for.

ISBN 978-0-06-232586-0

15 16 17 18 19   OV/RRD   10 9 8 7 6 5 4 3 2 1

Everything I do in my life, I do for Stacy, Nikki and Stephen. So, this book is for them, as always. And, as it is a book about fathers and sons, it is dedicated to my dad, Arnold, with all of my love.

"Just accept as a fact that everyone of any emotional importance to you is related to everyone else of any emotional importance to you; these relationships need not extend to blood, of course, but the people who change your life emotionally—all those people, from different places, from different times, spanning many wholly unrelated coincidences—are nonetheless 'related.'"

—John Irving, Trying *To Save Piggy Sneed*

My Father's Wives

I'VE BEEN STRUCK BY lightning several times.

Three, to be exact: once in high school, once in college, the last time afterward. None of them was my wife, by the way. You don't marry the girl who strikes you like lightning, because that doesn't last forever and you never know what you might be left with when it wears away.

I assume it goes without saying I'm not being literal about the lightning.

I mean it the way they did in *The Godfather*, when Michael first sees Apollonia: Italian countryside, exotic beauty who doesn't speak your language. That's the woman who hits you like lightning but you don't marry her, because life isn't in the Italian countryside, life is back in New York, where your brother is riddled with bullets under a toll-booth. And the girl you've fallen so hard for can't drive and doesn't speak English; good luck with that.

So, I didn't marry any of the women who struck me like lightning.

The first was when I was seventeen. Her name was Tabitha and she came to my high school after being kicked out of boarding school for sleeping with a teacher. She was gorgeous, flaming red hair and green eyes, and furthermore she was almost entirely unsupervised, coming and going as she pleased in a chauffeured limousine. She was a year behind me in school but light-years ahead in every other way. Long story short: there was a biology class, there were frogs floating stiffly in formaldehyde, she couldn't bear the smell, I dissected hers, and the next thing I knew we were having sex in the back of her car. It was in that limousine, with my school pants about my knees, that I first felt the lightning.

The second time struck a year later. I was a freshman at college and fell hard for a blond senior named Alyssa, who happened to be engaged to a medical student who lived hundreds of miles away. Alyssa toyed with me for much of the year, flirting, leading me on, allowing me to kiss her occasionally, no doubt driven by loneliness for her man and the pleasure she took in the way I worshipped her. Whatever the reason, I didn't really mind; I found her so fabulous I was just happy to be around.

Toward the end of the year I was invited by a sorority sister of Alyssa's to their formal dance and I accepted, even though I knew Alyssa and Phil would be there. I *wanted* to see them together, to put closure to it for myself.

The party was in the ballroom of a hotel, and several of the girls took a suite upstairs, away from the glaring eye of the university-designated chaperones. I was on a couch in the center of the suite, drinking Heineken from a bottle, while Alyssa seemed fidgety and sad and somewhat sloppily drunk. Then, it happened. When her fiancée got up to use the bathroom, Alyssa was quickly in my face, her nose an inch from mine. Her eyes were stunning—I can still picture them, vivid aquamarine—and despite her drunkenness there wasn't a streak of red. I could smell the alcohol on her breath too, sweet and fruity, as though she'd been drinking margaritas rather than the beer we had in the suite.

"Am I making you uncomfortable?" she asked breathily.

"A-a-absolutely," I stammered.

It was the opposite of what I meant to say, but I don't think she was listening. She just stayed like that for what seemed like an eternity, like time had stopped, her lips so near mine I could taste them, wet and sexy.

Then I heard a flush. The bathroom door opened, and as quickly as she'd come Alyssa was gone, out of my face and out of my life. That was the last time I ever saw her. She and Phil disappeared into one of the bedrooms and didn't come out the rest of the night. She graduated two weeks later. They were married within the year, and as far as I know they still are. But I can still see her eyes and smell her breath, and feel her lips not quite kissing mine. And when I do, it all looks and smells and feels like lightning.

The third time was in my early twenties with a model named Serena, who had a Jewish doctor for a father and an Indian mother who looked like a princess. The mother was stunning but drank like a fish and swore like a sailor, while her husband was patient and mostly silent, constantly monitoring his pager, ever aware of a pending emergency that never seemed to come.

From this bizarre union sprang Serena: Blue eyes and skin the color of the inside of a malted milk ball. And brilliant. She only modeled part-time; the other part she spent at NYU seeking a postgraduate degree in architectural engineering even though she had no interest in pursuing it. That was her problem, and ultimately her downfall: too many options. Women that beautiful and intelligent have an almost unlimited menu from which to choose, which sounds like a blessing but is often a curse because they can never commit to anything. For every choice they make there is always debilitating uncertainty over the options left on the table.

For a few months, Serena chose me. I vividly remember the first time I saw her, in Sheep Meadow in Central Park; I was playing Ultimate Frisbee, she was lying on a blanket. I chased an errant toss that landed a bit too near her and just as I began to apologize the clouds parted and it was as though the sun shone only on her, like a spotlight. The lightning stopped me in my tracks; I flung the disc back to my group and went immediately to her side. We had lunch and dinner that day and spent the night in her apartment, where in the candlelit stillness of her bedroom I said things so corny they sounded like lines from a movie you would walk out of.

Serena became an obsession. First, in a blissful way—I found myself whistling as I rode the subway. Then in an anxious way. And finally in a way that was just plain horrible. We had nothing in common. I was grounded, career-oriented, bursting with ambition; Serena was just bursting. Nothing satisfied her, not her studies, not her modeling career, and certainly not me. Her wanderlust bordered on maniacal. Once she told me how desperate she was to live in Asia; we were in a water taxi in Venice at the time.

We lived together for just over a year before she moved away, leaving me in her apartment, where I stayed until the lease expired. It was a damn nice place to live and a constant reminder of the great lesson of my youth: Lightning strikes are what they are, brilliant and flashy and electric, but also immediate, gone before the echo fades. To live in the reflection of the light seems exciting but ultimately is not a good idea. You're much better off finding a safe place and watching the storm through a window.

That's how I met Claire: Watching a storm through a window.

We were both leaving lunch in the same coffee shop when a sudden rainstorm took us by surprise; we found ourselves together under the awning, staring helplessly into the street. I was about to put my folded newspaper over my head and run three blocks to my office when she caught my eye, long and lean and elegant, hair darker than the black coffee in her Styrofoam cup. I wasn't struck by lightning. I just knew I wanted to talk to her.

She went back inside the coffee shop to wait out the rain so I did too, took the seat next to her at the counter and ordered coffee. I was trying to think of a witty way to introduce myself when her mobile rang.

"Yes, Liz," she said in an authoritative tone. "No, I haven't seen Mandy. I haven't seen her all week."

I couldn't hear the other end of the conversation. Behind the counter was a lot of shouting in Greek, and behind us waitresses snapped at customers to clear the way so they could deliver the omelets and grilled cheese sandwiches people were waiting for impatiently in crowded booths.

"I would love to help you, Liz," the classy brunette was saying, sounding exasperated, "but I haven't seen Mandy all week."

There was a bit more back-and-forth about Mandy, which seemed to make the attractive brunette increasingly annoyed, until she finally just said, "Okay!" and then abruptly hit *off* on her mobile without saying good-bye. She shook her head and then turned to find me staring at her, completely busting me; in the commotion I had forgotten we didn't know each other.

She didn't look put off, though. She just smiled. "I'm sorry if I was talking loudly, it's so noisy in here. I don't suppose you've seen Mandy, have you?"

"Actually," I said, "she came and she gave without taking, so I sent her away."

Her smile grew wider. She had very pretty teeth. "You don't hear people quote Barry Manilow every day," she said, and extended her hand. "My name's Claire."

We sat at that counter for three hours, long after the rain had faded and the lunch rush waned and all the tables turned over time and again; we sat and chatted and drank the cups of coffee the counterman kept refilling. There was no lightning. Just the opposite; it was as though we had known each other all our lives, two kids who'd grown up together and now met for lunch once a month to catch up. When she finally looked at her watch and said she needed to go, she jotted her phone number on the back of the check and shook my hand. I went to the window and watched her hail a cab. There was something very elegant in the way she moved, the cut of her tan raincoat, the way she slid into the back of the taxi. Clean and classy; as I went back to the counter to grab my briefcase, the sound of her voice echoed in my mind.

I smiled at the counterman. "Guess what, my friend," I said. "I just met the girl I'm going to marry."

He didn't congratulate me, or even smile. He just looked angry. Which I didn't understand until I looked at the check and saw that it was for one dollar; we had sat for three hours and ordered nothing but coffee. I folded a fifty-dollar bill into the palm of my hand and stuck it out over the counter. "Thanks very much," I said as we shook hands, "and guess what: you're going to forget me the minute I walk out that door, but I am going to remember you for the rest of my life."

It would have made a great line in a movie. Actually, if it had been a movie things would have progressed almost exactly as they did. We had a few dinner dates, she met my mother, I met her parents, then we went to Hawaii and I proposed over a candlelit dinner in a romantic restaurant while she struggled to stay awake, drowsy from anti-seasickness medication. It would have made the perfect cinematic montage, little snippets of a relationship growing and marching forward: the dates, the families, the wedding, the children being born. Then, when the credits finished rolling, the next scene would show the husband boarding a private jet. Just before takeoff, he would take out his iPhone and compose a very brief e-mail.

I came home early. I saw you.

As the jet picked up speed he would sit with his thumb hovering over the *send* icon. And as the plane lifted off the ground you would hear a voice-over, the husband narrating in a dispassionate voice.

"When I woke up that morning," he would begin, "my life was perfect."

Monday

WHEN I WOKE UP that morning, my life was perfect.

My alarm went off at 5:40; I was in my car ten minutes later and drove two miles to the train station, where I have the primo parking space that took years on a waiting list to acquire. It is not *a* primo parking space, it is *the* primo parking space; people in this town will be killing each other over it when I die. I got to the gym in Manhattan at quarter past seven and spent forty minutes on an Arc Trainer, watching Angelina Jolie talk about homeless children on the *Today* show. Then I went up to my office, still in sweat-soaked Under Armour. When my assistant saw me she picked up her phone and ten minutes later there was a toasted bagel, side of low-fat cream cheese, banana, and grande latte on my desk. I didn't see who delivered it. I was flat on the floor, stretching my lower back, reading the *Wall Street Journal*.

By nine I was through with the paper, my breakfast, and seventy-three e-mails that required immediate attention. I had also fired off a note to our IT staff to complain about the advertisements for penile enlargement kits that continued to sneak past our firewalls and into my mailbox. "Honestly," I wrote, "my six-year-old sent me an e-mail in which he said I stink like farts and *that* got rebuffed, but suggestions for becoming king of my bed by adding inches to my love life seem to be welcome. Can we do something about this?"

Bruce, the CEO of our firm, popped his head in the door just before ten. "What time today?" he asked.

"I'm ready now."

"Meet you there," he said, looking down at his tie. "I need to change."

Five minutes later I was in the elevator. My office is on the sixth floor; the basketball court is on nineteen. It's a terrific court: an abbreviated full court with regulation baskets on both ends and a three-point arc that stretches over the half-court line. It's the only place I've ever seen where you can play one-on-one on a full court, shooting at different baskets. Bruce designed it himself.

Bruce grew up playing ball in the city, just like I did. We figured that out in China the beginning of last year. Michael Jordan happened to be there at the same time, and his picture was on the cover of every newspaper. On the third day of our trip, Bruce looked at me and said: "I *really* feel like playing ball." We went out, bought sneakers, and asked the concierge to find us a court; we played two hours of one-on-one in a dusty elementary school gymnasium in Shanghai. It was a great day, for two reasons. First, it got me motivated to get back into shape. Second, and I guess more important, from that day on Bruce never went anywhere without me.

Since China we've played nearly every day that we are both in the office. Bruce is eleven years older than I am but he's still quick, and stronger than me and about four inches taller. But I can shoot the ball. Always could. Wake me up from a dead sleep and I can drain a sixteen-foot jump shot. When they tell you they can teach you to shoot they are lying; they can teach you the proper form, but either you can shoot or you can't, and if you can't then LeBron James could coach you and you'd never get really good. Bruce is a lousy shooter but he goes hard on the court; playing with him is about the best workout you'll ever have.

When we were done I went into the men's room, pulled my top over my head, and wrung it out into the sink. I loved the way I looked in the mirror. I hadn't been in this kind of shape since college. I took a shower and put on a navy suit, blue shirt, and lavender tie, then I went back to my office to talk to my kids. My daughter is nine, my son six. I have pictures of each of them facing me at my desk and almost every day I chat with them. I often don't see them at all during the week, even though we all sleep in the same house, because I leave too early and get home too late. Sometimes I catch Phoebe still stirring, so I kick off my shoes and get into her bed and she tells me stories about her day and her friends and her dance class and the tooth she is on the verge of losing and the type of dog she's decided she wants and the funny thing Drake said to Josh on television. Then she falls asleep on me, and I stroke her hair and watch her lips shudder and part, shudder and part. I seldom catch Andrew awake, but I love to go into his room and marvel at the impossible positions he manages to twist his body into beneath the covers. I swear, the child has never once slept a night vertically in his bed; he is always at some varying degree of diagonal, his arms splayed in one direction and his legs another. It always makes me laugh, no matter how long my day has been.

I miss them terribly during the week and I find that talking to them on the phone only makes it worse, so most days I speak to their photographs. That day, for instance, I recall saying something to Phoebe about how much I liked the dance number she was working on for the talent show, and I told Andrew how proud I was that he had dropped the bat halfway to first base in his T-ball game, which was a marked improvement from the previous time when he nearly decapitated an umpire. They are perfect, my kids. At least I think they are.

Now it was noon and the distant ache that talking to the pictures usually soothes was instead growing. I had been traveling too much of late; that goes along with being hoops buddies with the CEO. And we were going back to San Francisco that night, another night away, without even the pictures to talk to. So I decided to go home early, which I never do, but the hell with it; I needed to see the kids.

I had to sprint through Grand Central Station to catch the 12:37. I made my way to the bar car and ordered two beers, then stretched out and popped one open. I was unaccustomed to all the free space; coming home at rush hour the train is always SRO. Now I had it almost all to myself. On the other end of the car was a college girl drinking coffee, all spread out with books and bags and scarves. Midway between us were two blue-collar fellows with construction boots up on seats, talking too loudly about the Yankees. Aside from the bartender and me, that was it. The beer was crisp and tasted sweet. A calm feeling spread from my brain into my throat, down my chest, and all the way to my gut.

I was going to get home a little before two o'clock. Claire would be at a tennis lesson, then home to meet the school bus, only the kids wouldn't be on it. I was going to pick them up as a surprise and take them for ice cream, then we'd go home and my son and I would throw a ball around and my daughter would play Taylor Swift songs on her iPod, and it would be just like a Saturday except it was Monday. As I drove myself home from the train I was thinking this was a great idea, one of the best days I could ever imagine.

I burst through my front door in a hurry; I didn't want to be in a suit. I bounded up the stairs two at a time, headed to my closet to change. It was when I reached the top step that I first noticed something askew. Everything looked normal, but it didn't *sound* normal. There was a noise coming from the opposite end of the hallway that sounded both familiar and completely out of place at the same time. I started down the hall, loosening my tie as I passed the kids' bedrooms, both empty and quiet. The sound was coming from farther down the hall. There was only one more room on the floor, a guest suite where Claire's parents stay when they come to visit; they like that it is remote enough within the house to offer a bit of privacy. I don't know that I'd set foot in that room in a year. As I approached my heart began to slow down, even before there wasn't any question what I was hearing; my heart figured it out before my ears did. There was a keyhole in the door. I knelt, shut one eye, and when I looked in my heart almost came to a dead stop. What I saw was consistent with what I thought I had heard: a man and woman from behind, naked. He was pulling on a pair of jeans with no underwear beneath, long brown hair in a ponytail; I didn't recognize him. The woman I only saw for an instant, a flash of dark hair, before she disappeared from sight, headed toward the bathroom. I watched long enough to see the man sit on the edge of the bed, still facing away, putting on his shoes. I don't know why I didn't wait to see his face—of course I should have—or, more important, why I didn't confront them both right then. But I didn't. Watching him tie his shoelaces was already more than I could bear; I didn't want to see any more. I just stood up, opened my other eye, and dusted off my pants in the place where I had knelt. My mind was completely blank. My hands were beginning to shake. And my life suddenly didn't seem so perfect anymore.

MY FIRST THOUGHT WAS of the sheets.

I remember vividly the day we bought them. They're Frette, which is very fancy, and Claire and I got into an argument, first over how expensive they were, then over the pronunciation. Is it "fret"? Or the Frenchified "freh-tay"? I still don't know the answer. What I do know is the reaction I get from Claire if I approach the sheets while wearing shoes: it's as though I'm walking toward the Mona Lisa with a pair of scissors. She treats the sheets the same way my mother used to treat the good towels when I was growing up. The better towels were always in the guest bathroom, even though we never had any guests; they were all at my father's house. But that wasn't the point. The point is: I might have just witnessed the finish of my wife having sex with another man, and my first thought was of the sheets. The mind is funny that way. Oftentimes, the first thought it has is one that doesn't do you any good at all.

My next thought was that I was freezing. It was seventy degrees in the house but I was ice cold, shivering. There were so many things I could have done—should have done—but in that instant I didn't think of any of them. All I could think was that I needed to get warm. So I turned around and went back the way I'd come, out into the sunshine. I didn't look to see if Claire's car was in the garage, or any other car for that matter. Instead I just stood in the driveway and watched the postal truck as it rambled toward my house, paused at my neighbor's box, dropped off some mail, and rambled on. I don't know my mailman's name but he smiled and waved as he rambled toward my mailbox, opened it, dropped off my mail, and rambled on. I'm not sure if I waved back or not. On the lawn across the way, my neighbor's yappy little Jack Russell terrier was racing about in circles. The circles weren't consistent; sometimes the dog stopped and changed direction. I thought maybe it was chasing a butterfly. My neighbor's wife came down her driveway, wearing workout apparel and a pleasant smile. "Hey, Jon!" She looked down at the dog and shook her head; she knows the dog is a pain in the ass. "You're home early!"

"Yes," I said, and watched as she went to her box and fetched her mail, then snapped at the dog to behave and went back inside. The dog paid no attention; it went right on running in circles. I heard the whirring and clicking of a sprinkler kicking on, maybe even mine, I'm not sure. Someone's grass was being watered; it didn't really matter whose.

I was thinking of the day my grandfather died, when I was twelve years old. We were at the hospital, my mother and I, and I remember standing on the sidewalk on a busy street in Manhattan when it was time to leave, staring in amazement at all of the normalcy that surrounded me. How could the garbagemen and the shoemaker and the meter maid and the honking truck driver all be going about their business as though nothing was at all unusual? Didn't they know it was *not* a normal day? That's what I was thinking about while my postman was delivering mail and my neighbor's dog was chasing a butterfly and my wife and a stranger were getting dressed in my house.

I wasn't cold anymore. I just needed to see the kids. I was feeling so far from normal, I desperately needed normalcy; I needed my kids. So, rather than waiting for whomever it was to leave my house—or, better yet, slamming through the door and demanding answers—I did probably the least sensible thing I might have under the circumstances: I got into my car and drove away. I backed slowly out of the driveway, watched the mail truck and the dog running in circles in my rearview mirror until they disappeared from sight, then turned left on the main road and drove toward town.

The silence in the car was soothing for an instant, then it became deafening. It left me nowhere to go but inside my own head, which just then was not the best place to be, so I turned on the satellite radio, set to the channel that plays eighties music. Howard Jones was singing "Things Can Only Get Better." Down one notch to the seventies was "Don't Pull Your Love." I kept clicking around, trying to find a song that fit my mood, with no success. What I needed was a song that could turn time back ten minutes or so, and since no song can do that I finally just shut off the radio and drove to school.

I love visiting the school my children attend. I don't get there often, which may be part of the reason I so enjoy it. I find I feel peaceful and at ease when I am in the building no matter how loud all the children are when the bell rings; even the chaos is therapeutic. It reminds me not at all of the strict, competitive environment in which I was raised. My father insisted I attend the most elite New York prep schools, just as he had, a demand my mother honored even though he went out of our life the day I turned nine. My kids' school is nothing like that; it is a warm, nurturing place where the emphasis is on sharing and kindness. Claire occasionally voices concern that the school isn't academic enough, but nothing could worry me less. There will be ample time for all of that—eventually their entire lives will be all of that. Right now they are in fourth and first grades; let them be kids.

When I pulled into the parking lot I was still more than twenty minutes early. Instinctively, I reached over to the passenger seat, where my iPhone would be in the zippered pocket of my briefcase, only there was no phone. There was also no pocket, and no briefcase. Which meant my credit cards, driver's license, the *New York Times* sports section, a tube of Purell hand sanitizer, and a roll of Tums were all gone. I felt my face flush, a moment of panic; *this* was the last thing I needed. Visions of standing in line at the DMV flashed through my mind. But then, just as quickly, the answer came to me. The briefcase was not lost; in fact it had probably already been found. There was no question I was holding it when I went into the house, and equally little doubt that I wasn't when I left. I was sure the briefcase was inside, I just wasn't sure where. Though it didn't much matter. If it was destined to be found then it would be. If Claire stumbled over it she would, no doubt, be surprised and confused, which would make two of us; I'd deal with the briefcase when I got home.

I got out of the car and walked over to the playground. A few small kids were running around, none that I recognized. One, a little blond boy with too-long hair, was on his tummy on the ground; I think he was licking the grass. I wanted to grab him by the belt—if he was wearing one—and lift him out of the mess. But before I could, I heard a familiar voice.

"Daddy!"

There is no other word that sounds like that one does. And it never sounded quite as good as it did right then, on that playground, the sun shining on my face.

It was Andrew, age six, racing toward me, one shoelace untied, breathless. "What are you doing here?"

"I came to see *you*, of course," I said, and to my surprise my voice cracked.

I knelt and he ran into me, full speed, almost knocked me over backward. Phoebe was a few steps behind him, also running, though not quite as fast. Excited, though not quite as much. I wrapped my other arm around her and squeezed them both tight, buried my face in Phoebe's hair so I could smell her shampoo, like raspberries and a rainy day.

"What are we going to do?" Phoebe asked.

I cleared my throat. "Well, I had an idea," I said, my voice returned. "How about if we see if the ice cream shop is open on Mondays?"

Phoebe threw her arms up in the air and cheered, while Andrew, less certain, wrinkled up his nose as he does when he is thinking especially hard. "I'm not sure," he said. "I think I've only ever been there on weekends."

"Let's find out," I said, and took them each by the hand and walked jauntily toward the car, feeling marginally better. That's the thing about kids. They can't make all right a thing that could never be all right, but they can make it as close as it can possibly be. That's how I felt just then: as close to all right as I possibly could.

A few minutes later, after the short drive to the ice cream shop, during which Phoebe was ecstatic and Andrew was genuinely nervous that it wouldn't be open on a Monday, I made a discovery of an entirely different sort: I couldn't taste anything. I ordered soft-serve vanilla in a waffle cone with chocolate sprinkles and paid with the twenty bucks I keep in the ashtray for emergencies. On the first lick my thought was it didn't taste right, and on the second I realized it didn't taste like anything at all. This confused me because in *every* movie when a woman is wronged she turns to ice cream for consolation, and never once have I heard Sandra Bullock say: "You know, I can't even taste this." I tossed most of the cone in the trash. My son was delightedly licking chocolate from between his fingers; my daughter was wearing the contented smile of a nine-year-old who just got ice cream she wasn't expecting. Then we all piled into the car to drive home. And I assumed my life was about to change forever.

SO MANY THINGS HAPPEN in my house when I'm at work.

There are deliverymen with packages and lawn-care professionals with mowers and electric company inspectors with measuring gadgets and pool cleaners with long nets and Girl Scouts with cookies and religious nuts with pamphlets and the cable guy between noon and six and somebody's mom with a jacket my daughter left at a birthday party. I have always been a bit intimidated by the sheer volume of activity Claire manages around the house, though I suppose I'll never quite think about it the same way now.

I turned onto our street and saw Claire at the end of the driveway, poking through a magazine, the day's mail tucked beneath her arm. She was looking the other way, in the direction the bus would be coming from any minute. I reached in the glove compartment for my glasses, which I ordinarily only use for driving at night. I wanted to see her face as clearly as I could when she turned and saw me coming. Would there be anything there? A tick? A shudder? A moment of panic? I put the glasses on and took a deep breath, then tapped gently on the horn.

Claire turned, squinted, and stared, shielding her eyes from the sunlight with her hand, looking appropriately surprised. As we approached her face broke into a wide smile, and she began waving goofily at the kids, who both unsnapped their seat belts and leaned into the front seat, shouting.

"Daddy came home early!"

"We had ice cream!"

"Hi," I said, lowering my window. Claire walked right up alongside the car, looking perfectly normal. I hadn't any idea what to think. "How was your day?" I asked.

"My day is still going on," she said. "Is everything all right?"

Of course, that was the pertinent question. *Is everything all right?* I hadn't any idea what the answer was. My sense was everything was probably as far from all right as it could ever be. But I wasn't ready to say so. "I just missed everybody," I said.

"Now, *that* is nice," she said sweetly. And then, with enthusiasm, "Isn't it nice to have Daddy home?"

"Oh yeah, oh yeah, ohyeahohyeahohyeah!"

"It's lovely to have you home," she said, and leaned closer to kiss me, but I pulled forward into the garage before she could.

"I'll be back in a minute," I said as the kids rushed for their scooters. "I'm going to run inside and change."

I said that staring straight at Claire, certain there would be a signal of something in her face. Surely she would want to beat me inside, to straighten up, something. But there was nothing. She never diverted her gaze from the kids.

Alone, I went inside and up the stairs. For the second time that afternoon, I turned right instead of left, away from our bedroom and toward the guest room. The door was open, the French sheets in place, normal, crisp; they appeared clean. I couldn't bring myself to smell them, but there was no indication there would be anything out of the ordinary to smell. It looked the way the room always looks, the sheets looked the way they always do, the family photos on the nightstand in place, the four of us staring at me, smiling.

I considered, for a moment, that I was losing my mind. I hadn't experienced a hallucination since my sophomore year in college when I was talked into trying acid and spent three hours hiding under a blanket because I was absolutely certain the poster of Jimi Hendrix was breathing. I remember not knowing what to think back then, and now as I stared at a perfectly normal bed in a perfectly normal room, I didn't know what to think again.

I had an hour before a car would arrive to take me to the airport, so I changed out of my suit and into jeans. I was on the stairs headed back down when I heard The Police singing "Every Little Thing She Does Is Magic." That's the ringtone on my iPhone, which meant my phone was ringing and I could hear it. I looked downstairs toward where the music was coming from and saw my briefcase right in the center of the living room where I had dropped it an hour before. And, a few feet away, staring at it with a puzzled expression, was Claire. She didn't see me on the stairs, just heard the music and saw the briefcase, and her head dropped to the side, the way a dog's might when trying to make a decision. She had to be trying to decide why she hadn't seen me carry in the briefcase, wondering how it had managed to get from my car to the living room. Maybe she was trying to decide if I had seen her, if I knew. She looked worried. Not enough that anyone else would have noticed, but I know her really well. I know when she is worried, even if it is only a little.

When she finally shook her head and walked away, backward, into the kitchen, I found myself thinking of Hawaii and the night I proposed to her, both of us tipsy, she especially because the seasickness medication she had taken made her susceptible to the champagne. There came a moment when both of us knew it was time, a momentary silence across a candlelit table when our eyes met and there wasn't any question about it. Nor was there any question that I was the one obligated to begin, which I did, on my knee in a crowded restaurant. Twelve years later, alone at the top of the stairs, with the kids waiting outside, I decided this time it was Claire who was obligated to begin. Maybe she wouldn't get on her knee, but she would tell me.

I ran down the stairs and outside, grabbed a basketball, and shouted for Andrew, who came scootering across the driveway, followed by his sister. We were on the court for almost an hour and I remember none of it; I couldn't feel the joy of my children any more than I could taste the ice cream. All I could think of, through the yelling and the scootering and the slam-dunking, was my wife staring at the briefcase. Maybe she still was. Suddenly, without a word of explanation, I raced inside, leaving the two children alone. I needed to see if Claire was staring at the briefcase.

She wasn't.

I found the case exactly where I had left it and Claire nowhere near it. Was she upstairs, furiously laundering expensive sheets? Or in the bathroom, cleansing herself of whatever residue remained after an afternoon tryst? Or perhaps she was hidden in the attic where no one would find her, silently crying tears of remorse.

Then I heard the clatter of pots and pans and realized she was none of those places. She was behind me in the kitchen, rustling about in the drawer where the cookware is kept. It was a startlingly normal place for her to be and a startlingly normal thing for her to be doing; the only thing out of place was the briefcase.

You see, I know my wife as well as I know anyone. I don't claim to understand her, but I know her, which means while I cannot analyze most of the things she does, I can usually predict them. There is no way, under normal circumstances, she would ever leave my briefcase in the center of the living room floor. My wife is the sort who reminds you to put things away before you have even removed them from their place. If you say to her: "I think I'm going to watch a little television," she will reply with: "Sounds good, make sure you leave the remote control where you found it." She cannot, and does not, tolerate clutter. But now, she had made the conscious decision to leave my briefcase in the center of the floor where my children could trip over it or the dog could chew it up or a neighbor could see it and assume the household was in a state of abject chaos. That wasn't normal.

This was my chance to let her know it was time. "Honey," I shouted, as close to calmly as I was capable of. "Have you seen my briefcase?"

She was kneeling behind the island in the kitchen, still rummaging noisily among the pots and pans. Without looking up, she called back, "I think it's in the living room!"

"What is it doing there?" I asked accusatorially.

Claire stood, popping from behind the island like a magician making an appearance after having been sawed in half. "Where are the kids?"

"Shit," I said, and ran back out through the garage without another word.

If the children were surprised to have been left alone they didn't indicate it; they had just continued singing and slam-dunking and scootering as though I'd never been gone. We stayed outside and played until the familiar black Town Car pulled into the driveway.

Phoebe put her hands over her nose and smiled. That's her inside joke with me. The driver from the limousine service I use, Sonny, is dependable and friendly but has a bit of an odor problem. It doesn't bother me as much as it does Claire; the kids think it is absolutely hilarious.

What his arrival meant was that it was time for me to leave for the airport, so I took the kids inside for cold drinks. When we got to the kitchen, Claire was in front of the stove, warming olive oil in a pan.

"Wash your hands!" she yelled, adding, just for me, "That includes you."

I did. Then I got a bottle of water and two juice boxes from the refrigerator. And then, as casually as I could, I wandered into the living room without a word and saw that my briefcase was no longer on the floor.

WHEN I BOARDED THE jet I found Bruce stretched on the couch, watching basketball on an iPad, a silver tray of chocolate chip cookies balanced on his stomach. Bruce is a brawny man with voracious appetites, not limited to food, though he does eat as much as anyone I have ever seen. Since we began traveling together I have observed, with a combination of awe and disgust, that there is never a time when food is placed before him that he will not eat, and there is nothing discerning about his palate; from French truffles to Buffalo wings, Bruce will always partake. And, amazingly for a man of fifty-one, he pays no noticeable price.

There was a smile in my voice as I slid into the seat beside him and motioned toward the cookies. "You going to save any of those for me?"

"Have," Bruce said without looking up from the game. "There's plenty."

I shook my head. "You know the story of Dorian Gray? Somewhere in the world there is a painting of you as a very fat man."

Bruce still didn't look up. He is not the sort who cares if you give him a hard time. I can tell you a great many things about my CEO, some of them not so attractive, but the one thing I will always credit him with is supreme self-confidence. I have never seen Bruce express a shred of doubt in himself, his leadership, his athleticism, anything. He will eat and drink and buy whatever he wants, fight or fire or fuck whomever he wants, and never look back. He is like a shark in that way, more machine than beast, because of the singularity of his focus. He considers nothing and no one that interferes with his intentions and it's hard to argue with the results: Bruce is among the most power-ful executives on Wall Street, has unwavering support from his board of directors, and has to be worth close to a billion dollars. He also has a beautiful, doting wife who tolerates all of his indulgences, including the rampant infidelity of which she could not possibly be unaware.

"Who's playing?" I asked.

"Lakers," he said, still not looking up. Bruce consumes sports as voraciously as he does food, and wagers huge amounts on basketball and football.

I was trying to act normal. I wasn't feeling normal, but I was trying to behave as though all was well because I didn't want Bruce to notice. He is very hard to lie to, and I really didn't want to tell him I was pretty sure I had found my wife with another man.

I took out my iPhone and fiddled with it. "We waiting for anyone?" I asked.

"Just you," he said. "Should be wheels up in a few minutes. You want to watch this?"

"No, thanks," I said. "I need to respond to a few things."

The screensaver on my phone is a picture of Claire and the kids and me at Disney World. We had stopped at a stand where they painted faces and Phoebe wanted hers done but Drew, then only four, was afraid and would only do it if we all did. So in the photo my daughter has butterfly wings extending from her eyes, my son is Bozo the Clown, I have a tiger's stripes and fangs, and Claire is a fairy princess. It is the only picture I have on my phone; Phoebe e-mailed it to me and then made it my background. It always puts a smile on my face. Even now.

I opened a new e-mail and entered Claire's address. In the "subject" field I entered: *This afternoon.* Then I rolled the device about in my fingers, glanced over at Bruce, picked one of the cookies off the tray, and popped the whole thing in my mouth.

"Something to drink, Mr. Sweetwater?"

I had forgotten all about Sandra, our flight attendant, a delightful woman of about sixty, always cheery and deathly afraid of flying. She applied for the job when Bruce first bought the plane and he was taken by her sunny disposition and professional manner; it was not until the first time they hit a patch of turbulent air that her fatal flaw was revealed. I usually give Sandra a hug upon boarding but I wasn't myself this day.

"Would you like a drink?" she asked again sweetly.

I pointed apologetically to my mouth as I chewed the cookie.

"Perhaps a glass of milk?" she asked.

I swallowed. "Just some water," I said, rising, "and I'm sorry I didn't say hello—how are you?"

She gave me a quick hug, then pointed at the iPhone and shook her head. "Always too busy with *that* thing. You tell the boss here not to work you so hard."

I still hadn't quite decided what I wanted to say to Claire when I heard the engines roar to life. I sipped from the near-frozen bottle Sandra had brought and wiped my hand on my pants. My mind was racing and yet I was perfectly still. I could hear the roar of the engines, the reverberation of the fuselage. Sandra was taking her seat, strapping herself in, pulling her lap belt impossibly tight, crossing herself. I felt so empty it was like someone had sliced me open, removed all my organs, and sewed me back up again. There was nothing left inside.

I covered the screen of my iPhone with my left hand as I typed with my right, even though no one was around to see, nor would anyone, even Bruce, read over my shoulder. But there are some things you just don't take chances with, even if the chances are zero. I didn't want anyone to see the words I was typing. I didn't even want to see them myself.

I came home early. I saw you.

One of the two pilots, a pleasant, round-faced fellow whose name I never remember, stepped out of the cockpit. "We're ready to go, gentlemen," he said.

I nudged Bruce, who looked up from his game for the first time since I'd boarded. I pointed a thumb up in the air, and he nodded and shut down his iPad. Then he glanced up at the pilot and put his own thumb in the air.

The pilot disappeared again and I leaned back in my seat, closed my eyes. Bruce might want to chat now and I wasn't ready. Once we were in the air he could activate the satellite and watch the game on the television embedded in the front console; that would be just a few minutes. We were taxiing, my thumb hovering over the icon marked *send*. My eyes were closed, the engines roared in my ears, a faint aroma of jet fuel wafted through the cabin, and my head began to spin into what felt like a dream but was actually a memory. I was remembering the best night of my life.

Claire and I were on a beanbag in front of a fireplace, miles away, years before. A fire was crackling and the heat warmed my face, in the wonderful way that only follows a day of skiing in bone-chilling cold. We were in the Poconos, in Claire's parents' home, the night before Christmas. Three days later we would travel to Hawaii to celebrate New Year's. Five days later I would ask her to marry me. But that night, on that beanbag, drinking warm apple cider laced with rum, our feet digging into a white shag rug, Claire was talking about the two kinds of people in the world.

"There are those you lie *to* and those you lie *with*. At the end of the day, that's the most important distinction you can make. When you concoct a lie, am I in it with you? Or is it me you're lying to? If you promise always to lie with me and never to lie to me, I'll do the same."

Her face was so close to mine our noses touched, and I could smell the apples and cinnamon on her lips, feel the warmth of her breath. It was the closest I have ever been to anyone, in every way. It didn't feel like lightning at all—just the opposite. Lightning is loud and scary; Claire made me feel quiet and safe.

I took her hand in mine and held it to my face, kissed the tips of her fingers. They were chilled despite the heat of the fire. I put them to my cheek and pressed them against my skin. I wanted to promise her so many things. I wanted to tell her that I knew, from the first moment we met, that I needed to be with her, in the same way that I knew I needed to breathe to stay alive. I wanted to tell her that she made me feel as though I had spent my whole life looking in all the wrong places for all the wrong things, because it was clear to me now that so long as I could smell her breath and feel her frozen fingers on my face, then everything was all right and always would be. I wanted to tell her that all I needed in the world was for her to marry me. I would have proposed to her right there on that beanbag in front of that fire, but just then her mother walked in.

"My, look at you two," she said. "I can hardly tell where one of you ends and the other begins." She said it in a sweet way, as though she could feel at least part of what I felt. But if she had any inkling of what she was interrupting she didn't show it. She just dropped onto the sofa and breathed a heavy, exhausted sigh.

"He's a handsome one, isn't he, Mom?" Claire asked.

Her mother chuckled softly. "Oh, I'd say everything is about where it's supposed to be."

Claire was looking into my eyes as she spoke. "He's a sweet one too, isn't he?"

"He is," her mother replied. "But it's the sweet ones you have to watch out for, because they can get away with murder and they know it."

"Can you get away with murder?" Claire asked me.

"Probably," I said, "but I promise I will never try."

We both knew what I meant. Claire's smile was the softest I had ever seen. It said she was as comfortable as I was, that she knew everything I wanted to say. Not just then, but always. The way Claire looked at me said she knew better than I did what I felt and what I wanted, and that she had always known. Her face could say that to me back then. Sometimes it still does.

I would have asked her to marry me right there had her mother not fallen asleep on the sofa. Instead, it was five days later that we became engaged, but to this day I better recall the way I felt that night, by the fire, than I do when I knelt before her a few nights later. And I've always felt as though the promise we made to each other that night, to always lie together and never apart, was the most significant we ever made. It's a promise I've thought of often and never broken, not a single time in all these years. And I was always certain she hadn't either. Until today, when suddenly I wasn't certain of anything at all.

Then I heard the sounds of a basketball game on television, and I opened my eyes and found the game on the flat-screen. Bruce was again stretched out on the couch, a contented smile on his face, the silver tray of cookies balanced precariously on his stomach. I hadn't even realized we'd taken off, but as I looked out the window the lights below seemed a lifetime away. I looked over at Sandra, who was seated with her eyes tightly shut, mouthing what was surely a silent prayer.

I looked back to Bruce. "How long was I asleep?" I asked.

His eyes never left the screen. "Fifteen minutes. Maybe twenty."

I nodded. The iPhone was still in my hand. I entered my passcode and rubbed a finger over the face, clearing away a smudge from the screen. The words were crystal clear and seemed unusually bright.

I came home early. I saw you.

"No," I said aloud, though Sandra couldn't hear me and Bruce wasn't listening. "I'm not ready for that."

I hit the *delete* button and the words disappeared, instantly replaced by the Disney World picture again. There we were, the four of us, in face paint. We looked so happy, like the perfect family, an advertisement for Disney World. I stared at the picture as we ascended through the clouds, and quietly thought that I would have traded anything in the world just then to have been one of us.

WHEN WE LANDED IN San Francisco I was exhausted and Bruce was starving. Only one of those was unusual; I am almost never exhausted. Bruce is almost always starving, and one of the few drawbacks of traveling with the CEO is that when he is starving you eat, even if it is after midnight where you woke up that morning, back in the life you had before the afternoon changed everything.

We ate in the restaurant at the hotel, four-star French cuisine with a wine list roughly as long as the Old Testament. We were seated immediately, at a private table in the rear, and Bruce ordered Belvedere on the rocks and a Coca-Cola.

"I'll have the same," I told the waitress, "but hold the Coca-Cola."

Bruce smiled. He doesn't like to drink alone.

"You win?" I asked.

He knew I meant his wager on the Lakers game. "Won big."

I nodded as the waitress brought the drinks. "I'll drink to winning big."

Bruce clinked my glass with his, then looked up to the server. "Skip the Coke," he said, "and keep these coming."

Two hours later we had finished two sirloin steaks, baked potatoes, creamed spinach, a loaf of freshly baked bread, salads with Thousand Island dressing and a bottle of four-hundred-dollar Bordeaux. Bruce was leaning back, swirling the last of his wine in the glass. "This is where I really miss cigars," he said.

"You'll live longer," I said.

"I think I'd rather live shorter and smoke a cigar every now and again," Bruce said, a faraway look in his eyes. "They make me think of Brooklyn. My father loved cigars. Every night after dinner he would have a glass of brandy, and he would smoke a cigar and dip the tip of it into the brandy while he smoked." Bruce poked his finger into the glass. "He said it added flavor to the wrapper. My father was always working and he was always stressed out; he hated being poor and could never do anything about it. The only time I ever remember him relaxing was after dinner; he'd smoke his cigar and we'd talk about baseball."

"Which team? The Yankees?"

Bruce looked at me with horror. "My old man hated the Yankees. They were the enemy. My father's team was the Dodgers, the *Broooooooklyn* Dodgers."

"You aren't old enough to have seen the Dodgers in Brooklyn."

"No, I'm not," he said, still sloshing his glass. "But *he* was. He never got over them leaving Brooklyn. My mother used to say he started dying the day they left. Which would mean he started dying the year I was born." He paused, sucked the wine off his forefinger. "After the Dodgers left my father didn't have a team to root for, so after dinner we talked about how badly he wanted the Yankees to lose. He became obsessed with them losing. He didn't care who won, so long as the Yankees lost. If you asked which was his favorite team, my old man would say it was whoever was playing against the Yankees."

"At least you still had the time together," I said.

Bruce stared right in my eyes. "When you root for a team, you celebrate when they win," he said. "When all you do is root against one, there is only misery. My father took no satisfaction in seeing the Yankees lose. He said he did but he didn't, really. And he suffered when they won. There's nothing in the world worse than rooting for something not to happen, because if that's all you care about then all you can do is lose."

Bruce leaned back in his seat, still sloshing the wine in his glass.

He was looking away, out a window. "That's why I have never allowed myself to get attached to any team in my life," he said. "I love sports so I bet on every game to keep it interesting. But as far as emotionally, I couldn't care less."

I felt a familiar flutter in my stomach. Fathers are complicated for me. "And you got that from your dad?"

Bruce turned back. "Johnny, we get *everything* from our fathers."

I cringed. "Not me, unfortunately."

"Even you. Even if you didn't know him at all, you're still his son. Whether you realize it or not, you are just like him."

I shook my head vehemently. "No," I said. "In my case, I'm not."

"You *are*," Bruce said. "Listen, the one thing I remember most about my old man is how much he hated being poor. He used to say to me all the time, 'Brucey, we don't have a pot to piss in.' That was his big phrase: A pot to piss in. All I wanted was to get rich and get him the hell out of Brooklyn. I didn't make it. He died two years before I got to high school. But even after all that time, when I bought my mother her house on Long Island, I told the designer I wanted the word 'pot' engraved in gold on every toilet." He started to laugh. "He thought I was crazy."

"You bought your mother a pot to piss in."

"That's right," he said. "Because we are always our fathers' sons, whether we like it or not."

Bruce got quiet then, just finished the rest of his wine, and we called it a night. We had an early start in the morning and a long day ahead. I went upstairs, undressed, and then lay in the unfamiliar darkness of the hotel room, exhausted but unable to sleep. And what I found was that I was thinking more about my father than I was my wife.

THIS SEEMS AS GOOD a time as any to mention that my name is Jonathan Sweetwater, and yes, he was my father. Percival Sweetwater III.

Five-term United States senator, liberal lion, legendary lothario and bon vivant, author of nineteen books, sponsor of eleven legislative bills, trusted adviser to three presidents, husband to six women, and father to one boy.

That's me.

You are likely asking the same question I never got to ask him, which is: If he was Percival the third, why wasn't I Percival the fourth? I didn't ask him because I never saw him again after my ninth birthday party. But, fortunately or not, he was asked the question by his chosen biographer.

"I didn't name my son Percy," he was quoted as saying, "because, let's face it, there could never be another one like me." It wasn't made clear in the book if he was kidding, or even smiling, when he said it. Knowing what I do of him I'd say it's likely he was not.

I was born when my father was in his forties and still on his first wife, my mother, Alice, of whom he told the press on their wedding day: "She puts the 'sweet' in Sweetwater." It was a line he would use five more times, with each of his subsequent wives, and with no hint of apology. When reminded by reporters that it wasn't the first time he had used the phrase, his stock response was: "In life, as in Congress, we rarely get things right the first time." With women, Percy continued trying to get it right throughout his life. When it came to children it seems he gave up after me.

On the rare occasion that a reporter contacted me I too had a stock reply, which never failed to generate a laugh. "Mother's Day," I would say, "has always been my most expensive day of the year." It was funny, but it wasn't true. Of my father's six wives, I only ever met two. And apart from my mother, I haven't been in touch with any of them in thirty years. But that doesn't make the line any less funny. I learned that trick from my father too: another of his stock comments was "Percy Sweetwater never lets the facts get in the way of a good story."

How, you may wonder, did a man so brazenly self-indulgent manage to ascend to such a towering place in society? The best answer I ever got to that question came from my mother, who had more reason than anyone to bad-mouth Percy but never did. "Say what you will about your father," she told me, "but at least he was his own man. He was unapologetically, unequivocally, unreservedly himself. And in the world we live in today, people respond to that." I always thought she might have been talking more about herself responding to Percy than anyone else, but either way it remained that Percival Sweetwater III was a treasured figure in American politics.

When my father died, the *New York Times* eulogized him as THE LAST LION. The funeral was covered by CNN, MSNBC, and all the major broadcast networks; I saw the satellite trucks parked outside the church on Fifth Avenue. In fact, they were *all* I saw. I didn't get into my father's funeral. I was invited, but I managed to misplace the invitation somewhere en route from my apartment, a mistake my mother called "the ultimate Freudian slip." I tried to explain to the security guards outside the church doors that I was the son of the deceased, but it was very much like trying to talk your way past the bouncers guarding the velvet rope at a nightclub: they were listening to me, but they couldn't have cared less what I was saying.

I watched from across the street as two former U.S. presidents entered the church. Then I went into an Irish pub, ordered corned beef and cabbage, washed it down with four beers, and watched the coverage on television. Then I went into the men's room, threw it all up, rinsed my mouth and face with cold water, and went to the office.

When I told my mother what happened she responded by giving me a gift. It was a car, with vanity license plates. NOT IV. She said that was the perfect sentiment for me to express to the world as I passed it by. It wasn't especially funny but I laughed anyway. That's the way it works when you have a famous father to drive away from: you make jokes even though there really isn't anything funny at all.

TUESDAY

UPON OUR RETURN FROM San Francisco, where the business went well and the basketball was especially spirited, I lingered on the jet. I am usually up before the door is open, my belongings gathered, with just a quick hug for Sandra and nod to the pilots before I am off, down the stairs to where the familiar Lincoln Town Car is idling.

But that evening I was in no such hurry. Bruce was up and about, and Sandra had unbuckled her seat belt and sent her blessings for a safe landing skyward, and the pilots were in the rear of the aircraft gathering their wheeled suitcases, and I hadn't budged. I wasn't quite sure what would happen when I got home, and I wasn't in any rush to find out.

Bruce patted me on the shoulder. "I'm going into the city," he said. "See you in the morning."

Sandra gave me a squeeze about the neck. "Isn't it wonderful to be home, Mr. Sweetwater?"

The pilots were milling about, checking their watches and clearing their throats, looking forward to dinner or a gym or a woman or wherever it is pilots go when the flying is done. I couldn't think of any way to further delay the inevitable.

And then I did. "Bruce! Wait!" I unbuckled my seat belt and hurried for the door.

Bruce was going to "the city." I knew what that meant. His home isn't in the city. Home, for Bruce, is in Greenwich, with the other Wall Street billionaires. "The city" is where his other life is, namely a penthouse in the residences of the St. Regis Hotel, a perk he negotiated into his contract and takes full advantage of. That was where Bruce was going, and god knows who would be waiting when he got there and what they would do. But he was always inviting me to do it with him and that night, for the first time, I found the idea appealing.

"Afraid he's gone, Mr. Sweetwater," one of the pilots said. "As always it's been our pleasure to get you home safely and we look forward to seeing you again real soon."

Outside the air smelled fresh and there was a chill in it, a good chill, the sort that awakens the senses after a long flight. What there was not, however, was the Lincoln Town Car. In all the years Sonny had been my driver he had never been late; perhaps he stopped at a gas station to pick up some of that cologne he thought masked his body odor. I was just thinking I would have to bust his chops good-naturedly when I saw a car pull out onto the tarmac, but it wasn't the Lincoln Town Car. It was a Range Rover. So it wasn't Sonny.

It was Claire.

THERE IS AN INN in Vermont where Claire and I like to go. We joke that it is as far from civilization as you can be while still able to get a decent bottle of wine. In fact, the wine is better than decent, it is legendary, as is the inn itself among foodies. Tucked safely away from the ski resorts that attract the wildest and loudest of crowds, our inn is not for skiers, it is for those of us whose preference on a snowy day is a casual stroll, a good book by a fire, and world-class food and drink.

We discovered our Vermont getaway during the first winter of our marriage, when Claire's parents insisted over dinner in the city that we join them for a weekend in the same ski house where we had almost gotten engaged.

"We can't this weekend, Dad," Claire said, and put a hand on my knee and squeezed. "We're going up to Vermont with friends."

Her smile came so easily, so casually, there was no way anyone could have guessed we had no such plans. It was a bald-faced lie. I remember I marveled at the coolness of her dishonesty; rather than see it as a sign of danger, I loved it. Her hand on my knee meant she was doing exactly what she promised she would: lying *with* me, as opposed to *to* me.

Later that night, at home, I asked why she had lied to her parents.

"I hate skiing!" Claire said. This was stunning coming from a woman with whom I'd had to ski constantly during our courtship; I'd been dragged to her parents' house in the mountains countless times so I could behold her effortless grace while I mostly just hoped for the sensation to return in my toes.

"You're kidding," I said. "I hate it too! I thought you loved it."

"Never! My parents have been making me ski since I was six; I've hated every day of it. It's freezing cold, the lift lines are endless, and the food in the lodge is disgusting, even the hot chocolate. I just never had the heart to tell my parents because it makes them so happy. But come on, I'm a married woman now."

I think every couple has that perfect moment, when both people realize they really are right for each other and all the assumptions they had to make along the way have been verified. Little doubts melt away, and for the first time they both know for sure they really are going to be all right after the euphoria of the engagement and the buzz of the parties and the whirlwind of the wedding and the sporadic arrival of fancy dishes; when life becomes just life again, they really are going to love each other after all. For Claire and me, that was our moment. We embraced like we had never embraced before and made love on the floor. Afterward we sat in our underwear and drank tea and searched the Internet for the name of a Vermont inn we could give to her parents to complete our lie.

As it turned out we found a place that sounded so delightful, so far from the hectic squalor of the slopes, that we decided to try it, and we loved it and have spent at least one weekend a year there ever since. And every time we go, at least once during the visit, often while savoring the last remnants of a particularly piquant Burgundy, I am reminded of how casually and artfully Claire began the whole thing, how naturally the deceit had come to her. How easy the smile had been on her lips, and the steadiness of her breathing, the certainty of her eyes. And the stillness of her hands.

That is one thing about my wife that is remarkable: her stillness. There are some people who are naturally jumpy, constantly tapping their feet or jiggling their legs or rustling their fingers; Claire is the exact opposite. Her hands never move. It is an amazing quality, one you would not notice until you became aware of it, but once you do it never ceases to draw your attention. It was in Vermont that I first noticed her hands, at the dining table, resting ever so gently on a folded linen napkin, graceful, slender, perfectly still. There is something in her stillness that suggests everything is all right. Which, if you know Claire, it usually is.

So, as I watched the Range Rover circle around the rear of the aircraft and stop beneath the stairs, my first thought was that I needed to see her hands.

The window went down and Claire looked up at me with a crooked smile on her face. "Surprise!" she shouted. "How's this for service?"

"Very nice." I couldn't quite manage to return the smile. "To what do I owe the pleasure?"

"Well, did you want to spend your fortieth birthday with your wife or your driver?"

"Isn't that tomorrow?" I said. I had been so preoccupied I had completely forgotten my birthday, my fortieth no less. Although, we don't normally make too much fuss over birthdays anyway. The day I turned nine was the worst day of my life. Since then, I haven't had much appetite for celebration.

"This is close enough," she replied. "Come on, let's go have dinner!"

"How about the kids?"

"I got a babysitter, they're fine."

"But I won't see them tonight, and I've been gone so long."

Claire shook her head. "Jonathan, you've been gone one day. The kids are fine. Let's go to Angelo's and have some fun."

Angelo's is our favorite spot: Italian, great food, charming owner who always greets me with a kiss on both cheeks and a bottle of Pinot Grigio on ice. I love Angelo's, but I was in no mood to go out.

I stepped carefully down the stairs and kissed Claire as quickly as I could. Her lips were dry. Usually they were not. Backing away, I darted around behind the car and slid into the passenger seat.

"Not much of a kiss," Claire said.

"Sorry." I wanted to say more but I didn't know what. Hadn't I read somewhere that dry lips are a sign of nerves? I needed to see her hands.

Claire regarded me skeptically. "Everything go okay in California?"

"Fine, I'm just a little tired. I'm going to close my eyes a few minutes if you don't mind."

"I don't mind," she said, but didn't look like she meant it. She looked like she minded a great deal. She looked as though my being tired was causing her great distress.

"Unless there's something you need to talk to me about," I said. Every muscle in my body clenched. There are few moments like that in life, when absolutely everything hangs in the balance. I braced myself for it, whatever *it* was. I felt like I had been living with it for too long to bear, even if it had only been a day.

"No," Claire said. She turned away from me, put the car in drive, and drove toward the exit, following the lead of a man in a yellow plastic vest. "Nothing out of the ordinary. I just wanted to celebrate a little. Are you too tired to go out?"

She wanted to go to Angelo's. It seemed important to her. Maybe she needed a drink to build up her nerve, or maybe she wanted to tell me in a public place where I would have to maintain my composure. If that was how it had to be I would go, because I needed her to tell me. I couldn't carry this another day. If she needed to go to Angelo's, I would go.

"I'm fine," I said. "I'll just close my eyes a few minutes."

I pressed deeply into the headrest and let my hands fall by my sides. My eyes really did feel heavy. The hum of the engine was soothing, and when Claire pulled out onto the highway the ride was smooth. I cracked the window a bit and the air was cool and smelled fresh. I took a deep breath and felt my head settle gently onto my shoulder. Perhaps a few minutes' sleep was just what I needed. It was only twenty or so to the restaurant. My entire life might change when we got there; I might as well rest while I still could.

Then, ever so softly, I felt a hand resting on my thigh. I opened one eye just enough to see the creamy white of Claire's skin, the flash of a diamond, soft pink nail polish. I looked up at her face and she looked back and smiled sweetly. "You rest," she said, and patted my leg.

I yawned and rested my head back on my shoulder. A warm, dizzying wave rushed over my brain, and I think I was more asleep than I was awake when I realized something was wrong. I opened my eyes once more and looked down and instantly knew what it was. Claire's hand was trembling. Not a lot, but enough. I closed my eyes again. It hurt too much to look.

When the car stopped my head jerked away from the window. There was an ache in my neck from the uncomfortable position in which I'd slept. I looked over at Claire and there was no doubting it now: there was anxiety in her eyes.

"Shall we go in?" she asked in a voice I could tell was trying to sound natural.

I sighed. "I suppose we should."

I would leave it to her from here. However she would raise it, whenever she was ready, whatever she had to say, I would listen. Of course I had questions; I would probably always have questions. But first, I just wanted to hear what she had to say.

Claire took my hand as we walked through the parking lot and I could feel her palm was clammy. Claire's palms are never clammy, just as her hands never tremble. Everything was wrong. It was as though I didn't even know her. This couldn't continue. I was just about to stop and demand to know what in the hell was going on when a strange thing happened: In the reflection of the restaurant window, I saw my daughter's face.

Phoebe was smiling, that wonderful crooked smile she inherited from her mother, where it's as though a light has been turned on inside of her. The only explanation I could think of was that I was having a breakdown, hallucinating, here outside the window and perhaps in the house as well. Was it possible I had imagined all of it? The noises in the bedroom, the man with the ponytail, my daughter in the window; were they all in my mind? That is what I was wondering when I came out the other side of the revolving door.

And then I saw my mother.

She was seated in the first booth on the right, with Phoebe beside her, looking out the window. Across from them both, sucking on a maraschino cherry dangling from a stem, was our friend Betsy Buchanan, who looks so much like Claire I once mistook her for my wife and fondled her behind. I shook my head at the madness of it all. Then I looked up to find Andrew running toward me at top speed. Behind him was Angelo, beaming with his arms open wide. My friend Simon and his family were behind them, and all around me were faces I recognized, even Bruce, and Sandra, the flight attendant, with a bottle of beer in her hands. And then, just as Angelo reached out and grabbed my face with both hands, I realized what was happening.

"SURPRISE!!!!!!!!!"

I turned to Claire as Angelo kissed me on both cheeks, and she was laughing with tears in her eyes. Her mother was handing her a glass of wine, and music was playing and everyone was cheering and I was being pulled backward and I realized it was Andrew so I scooped him up in one arm and squeezed him hard. Phoebe arrived next and I got on one knee and hugged her with my free arm while holding her brother in the other. "Happy birthday, Daddy!" they both said, again and again.

I stood up without letting go their hands, which felt warm and sticky. My mother gave me a kiss. Betsy Buchanan rubbed her hand against my cheek, smiled mischievously, lingered an instant too long. "Happy birthday, you handsome devil," she said.

"All right, everybody!" Angelo yelled above the din in his heavy Italian accent. "The celebration begins! Let's eat!"

The music turned louder as Bruce approached carrying two drinks. He handed one to me. "Happy birthday, big fellow," he said.

"Belvedere?" I asked.

"Damn right."

I took a long sip. It was cold and the lime was refreshing. "How long has this been going on?"

"I've known at least a month," Bruce said. He motioned at Claire. "She worked hard on this. Just about drove me crazy with scheduling, but she did a good job."

I took another long sip, finished the drink, motioned to Angelo that I needed another. "A month?" I asked, turning back to Bruce. "She's been putting this together for a month? How did she keep it from me?"

Bruce put his arm around my shoulders. "My friend, you *are* a little oblivious sometimes."

"Am I?"

Bruce roared with laughter. "Come on, I'm busting your balls. She kept it from you because that's what women do." Angelo handed me another drink, and Bruce tapped me on the cheek. "Here's Helen," he said.

Bruce's wife smiled sweetly and tugged at the sleeve of his shirt. "Come on, now, just because you're the boss doesn't mean you get to monopolize the birthday boy."

I leaned across and gave her a kiss. "Thanks for coming."

"We wouldn't have missed it," she said.

Bruce still had his arm around me. "Johnny can't believe Claire managed to pull this off without his having any idea," he said.

Helen smiled again. "Your wife is something else," she said. "I don't think there's anything she couldn't pull off if she set her mind to it." Then she turned to Bruce. "Now, you leave him alone and let his friends give him a hug."

Bruce pounded me on the back. "Have fun tonight," he said, and the two of them disappeared into the crowd. Knowing Bruce, they were headed for the bar.

I took another long drink and surveyed the room. It really did appear everyone I knew was here. Even my neighbor with the yappy little dog. Claire must have worked hard to pull it all off, and without my suspecting a thing. Couldn't help but make me wonder what else she could pull off, as Helen had said, if she put her mind to it.

Then another hand was on my shoulder and I recognized it from the touch. Claire always comes from behind me, gently laying her fingers on my neck. I closed my eyes and focused on her hand against my skin. Was it still trembling? Was it still clammy?

"I thought I was going to lose it completely in the car," she said.

I turned to face her. She was Claire again. I mean, *really* her. Not the stranger who was so anxious before, with trembling hands and damp palms. This was my wife. The woman who could keep anything a secret from me but promised she never would.

"Thank you," I said. "This is great."

She frowned. "You don't look happy."

"Just a little overwhelmed."

She leaned close and kissed me on the lips. Hers weren't dry anymore. "Enjoy," she said. "Everyone is here because they love you."

Then she turned to greet another guest, I think a teacher from school. I caught Angelo's eye and he walked over, holding a filled glass in his hand. "You look like you need another one of these," he said.

I smiled. "My friend," I said, "you have no idea."

WEDNESDAY

WHEN I WOKE UP the sun was shining.

I was sure I had set the alarm but clearly Claire had turned it off, in fact yanked the plug out of the wall; the digits were flashing midnight. She would never have done that if she hadn't spoken to Bruce about it. It was a statement, from them both, that I needed the rest. Neither of them knew just how right they were, or why.

In my closet, I pulled my iPhone out of my jacket, which was hung sloppily on the door. Ninety-four e-mails. Those would have to wait. I typed a quick note to Bruce. *Slow start today. Hoops a little later than usual.* Then I went into the bathroom and switched on the radio by the sink. It was tuned to the news station for weather reports and headlines, but I didn't want those. I clicked from AM to FM in search of music and found an old Motown tune I like, even though I always get most of the words wrong.

I was in the shower singing Motown, clearing shampoo from my eyes, when I saw her: Claire, outside the shower door, naked. I could barely see for the steam that fogged the glass, but I recognized the look. Claire doesn't often initiate but when she does it is usually pretty creative, like this, much better than what I do, which is grab or grope her at the least realistic times, like when the kids are playing in the kitchen or company is expected in ten minutes or her parents have just visited. Now she was outside the shower, naked, and all I needed to do was open the door.

But I could not.

I could spend a lot of time trying to explain the reasons I could not and probably still not fully understand them all myself, but in the end that didn't make much difference. Sometimes you only need to know one thing for absolute certain and right then I did: No matter what, I could not open that door.

So I had a dilemma. If I rebuffed an offer this brazen it would make a statement I wasn't sure I was ready to make; I was not prepared to have Claire think I never wanted her to do this again. I didn't know where this day was leading, but if Claire was going to continue to be my wife I wanted her to be naked and smiling outside the shower as often as possible. What I needed was a way to push this moment off until I could further figure things out. So, I did the only thing I could think of. I opened the shower door, stuck my head out, made my face as miserable as I could, and said in a sickly voice: "Honey, I was throwing up half the night!" And just like that, it was done. I had broken the most important promise I ever made.

Meanwhile the look on Claire's face changed immediately, and just as quickly she was gone. If there is one thing my wife cannot handle it is vomit. One time Phoebe contracted a stomach virus and Claire nearly moved out of the house. Like the dutiful mother she is, she cleaned up around her daughter, but she wore a surgical mask and rubber gloves, and even so she herself threw up after every cleanup.

If you had told me two days ago that I would be lying to my wife in order to get out of having sex, I would have said you were deranged on both counts. But there I was, in the shower, water scalding my neck and shoulders, lying and alone. And in no mood anymore to sing along with the music.

FIFTEEN MINUTES LATER, DOWNSTAIRS, Claire was at her writing table flipping through a magazine. She frowned when I entered wearing a suit and leaned away when I approached her. "What are you doing?" she asked.

What I was doing was getting out of the house. My head ached from the vodka and the confusion. I knew I had decisions to make and questions to ask, but I wasn't in any condition to ask them.

"Jonathan," she said when I didn't reply quickly enough, "get *back* into bed."

"I can't."

"Are you kidding? You're *sick*! Don't even think about going anywhere except to bed. I'll bring you up something to eat if you want."

"I have a meeting I absolutely cannot miss," I said. "If I was shot in the leg I would have to hop into the office, *that's* how important it is."

Lying, again. So easily, in fact, that I felt unnerved; breaking life-long promises shouldn't be quite so unmonumental.

Claire still looked skeptical. "I don't think I like this."

"I'm fine," I said. "A little run-down and too much vodka at the party, but the sleep helped and now I actually feel hungry."

Claire looked me up and down, then nodded slowly. "Okay, I'll make you some toast," she said. "That's what you need, dry toast and a banana."

"And coffee."

"I'm making you *tea*," she said, and smiled faintly. "I need you better."

I sat down at the table and took out my iPhone. So many e-mails. "How were the kids this morning?" I asked.

Claire was watching the toaster. We have the world's slowest toaster, but she insists the quality of the toast is worth the patience. "Adorable," she said. "They were so excited to look at all the pictures from the party."

I felt a pang in my side, the rueful mourning of something fun that I missed. I am acutely aware that Phoebe will only be nine for so long, and Andrew six. Every day that passes, every laugh I miss, is gone forever. "Where's your phone?" I asked.

Claire turned away from the toaster with a puzzled expression. "What?"

"I want to look at the pictures."

Her expression did not change. It was difficult to describe the look. I wouldn't call it panic and I wouldn't call it guilt, but I'm not sure there is a better word either.

"What's the matter?" I asked, trying to sound casual. "I'm not allowed to see your phone?"

The toast popped. "You know I just can't handle how sick you were last night," Claire said, lifting the bread with her fingertips and dropping it onto a plate. "I'll e-mail you the pictures. What time is your meeting?"

"One this morning, another late in the afternoon."

"I think if you absolutely have to go then you should spend the night in the city."

A chill ran down my spine. *The city.* I forgot all about the phone.

"You need to rest," Claire continued. "When you're done with your meeting just get a hotel room, order room service, and go to bed. You don't need to be on the train surrounded by all those people or in a car in ridiculous traffic."

"Maybe I will," I said, picking my iPhone up from the table. "Maybe I will."

I opened an e-mail, typed in Bruce's name. *You in the city tonight??*

His reply came in less than a minute. *Can be. You in?*

I took a bite of the toast. *Can be. You up for it?*

This time it wasn't fifteen seconds. *You bet your ass.*

"WHY CAN'T YOUR DAD clean his own windshield?"

That was the seminal question of my childhood. At least, it is the first of its kind I can recall being asked, and it was followed by more than I could keep up with, but you always remember your first.

What I remember most is not how it made me feel, but how my mother made me feel about it. Really, it is *that* which is most significant about the whole thing; it was the first time I recall my mother explaining life to me in a way that made it seem less daunting.

It was Lee Marshall who asked the question, at Yankee Stadium. Lee was the prettiest girl in our second-grade class, which at the time meant nothing to me at all. She was also the daughter of one of the richest men in New York, Robert Marshall, who traveled about the city in the back of a Rolls-Royce. Lee's father's wealth was of no import to me at age seven either; I was just impressed by his Yankees tickets.

Lee invited me to join her family in their box seats for a game during the World Series. We rode in the back of Mr. Marshall's limousine, me in my Yankees jacket and matching hat, Lee in a dress you might wear to a dance. It was game six, which proved to be among the most famous in history: Reggie Jackson slammed three home runs and the Yankees clinched the championship. But what I remember most, amid the din that only fifty thousand New Yorkers can create, was Lee turning to me and saying: "My daddy says your dad wants to take all of our money and give it to the men who clean the windshields when you stop for red lights. Why can't he just clean his own windshield?"

Reggie Jackson hit his historic third home run right after she asked that. We joined the crowd in a standing ovation, and when the game resumed Lee had forgotten all about the question. But I didn't forget. Even as I watched the Yankees spill out of their dugout to celebrate, I couldn't get the question out of my head. I didn't know the answer, but I knew who would.

"Your dad is a powerful man," my mother told me that night at home. "Powerful men make decisions they believe in and stand up for them, even when other people criticize them. So you can feel proud to know that your father stands for something, even if some people don't like it."

"Do they not like him?" I asked.

"It's not him," she said. "Every one of the men who disagree with your father would love him if they sat down together. They just disagree with his positions."

I have since come to know that at the time of this conversation, my father was already involved in a relationship with the woman who would become his second wife, and my mother knew it.

"I don't understand," I said that night. "Why does Lee's father care if Dad washes his own windshield?"

"He doesn't care about your father's windshield, he cares about his own," my mother said. "Your father believes that people like Mr. Marshall, who have a lot of money, should pay some of that money in taxes so that people who have less can afford to live. Like those men in the street who wash the windshields. Do you understand?"

"I think so."

"Does that seem fair to you?"

"I don't know."

"That's right, because you're seven years old and all you should care about is that your favorite team won the World Series. Don't let things you don't understand interfere with your fun. Remember that the next time anybody mentions your father."

I still remember it today. Just as important, I remember that when I am in trouble it is invariably my mother who can make things better. So, on my fortieth birthday, nursing a miserable hangover (I wasn't lying about that), I rode a later train into the city and took the subway downtown to see my mother.

The apartment she lives in is the same place where I mostly grew up; with my father we lived on Central Park West, but when he went his way we went down to Sullivan Street, where we were surrounded by the artists and beatniks among whom my mother felt much more comfortable than she did the power-and-politics set uptown. She loved telling people we lived on the street that Bob Dylan used to live on, which was true. My mother loves Bob Dylan. "In his lyrics," she says, "you can find the answers to just about anything." I listened to Dylan on my iPod all the way into the city that day, but nowhere in his songs could I find what a man is supposed to do when the only promise he really cares about has been broken.

I picked up two steaming lattes and two chocolate croissants from the café on the corner of MacDougal and Bleecker streets. Not from Starbucks. Never Starbucks for my mother, who began bemoaning the loss of identity of her beloved neighborhood the day they opened the Banana Republic on Sixth Avenue. When I rang the bell I could hear yoga chimes behind her voice over the intercom. "Surprise," I said.

"I've been expecting you," she replied. "Hold on."

A moment later I heard the cavalcade of locks on the door being turned, one by one. A crank, a click, a slide—nine in all, the same nine locks that have guarded that door since 1978. The sounds they make, in the order my mother opens them, are burned into my memory.

After the ninth lock, a lengthy, crackly slider, the door flew open and I found my mother exactly as I expected her: bare feet, yoga pants, baggy T-shirt, headband.

"Chocolate?" she asked, pointing at the paper bag.

"Absolutely."

"Can't resist that," she said, and took the bag from beneath my arm. "Now, what the hell is going on with you?"

The apartment smelled of burning incense and espresso, and from the old-fashioned stereo came the chimes and sounds of the ocean that my mother listened to on cassette while she did her yoga. I pointed toward the mat in the center of the room. "Did I ruin this?" I asked.

"I was just about done," she said. "Do you want to do some sun salutations with me?"

"No, thanks."

"You want a decaf espresso?"

"I brought lattes," I said. "In the bag."

"Yum." She sat at the kitchen table, pulled a croissant from the bag, and took a bite without a plate or napkin, just a hand beneath her mouth to catch the crumbs. "Oh, that is just delicious," she said, and took the top off one of the lattes, held it up to her face, and inhaled deeply. When she looked up, a tiny bit of foam was on the tip of her nose.

I sat across from her and pulled the other croissant from the bag, took the biggest bite I could, and felt the warm chocolate ooze in my mouth. Delicious. I took another bite.

"Jonathan," my mother said. "Put that down and finish chewing."

I smiled, laid what was left of the croissant on the table. "Like I'm still eleven years old."

"Not like that at all," she said. "When you were eleven years old I was concerned you were going to choke. It's obvious to me now that you can manage to eat without killing yourself, but that doesn't mean you have any idea what eating is for. If all you're doing while you are chewing is waiting to take another bite, then you aren't experiencing what you're eating. You're eating just to eat. Something like *this* is meant to be experienced."

I looked down at the table. I had almost none of my croissant left. Mother had taken just the one bite and was licking the flaky crumbs from her hand.

"I need to talk to you about something important," I said.

"I'm not in a hurry if you're not."

I nodded and took a sip of my latte. "I have reason to believe that Claire may be having an affair."

AFTER I HAD TOLD her all I could think of to tell, and all the croissants and coffee were finished, my mother looked across the table at me with a serious face. "So, you were outside the door?"

"Yes."

"You didn't go in the room?"

"No."

"You didn't *actually* see her?"

"I don't know."

"You don't know what?"

I shook my head. "I don't know what I don't know. I saw someone. It looked like her. I think I was in shock; maybe I still am." I put my elbows on the table and laid my head in my hands. "I have this horrible, empty feeling. And I'm scared to death to confront her, because I feel like if it's true then I'm going to have this feeling for the rest of my life."

Mother made her face even more serious. "Jonathan, I understand what you're saying. And I know how difficult confrontation is for you. But unless you are going to tell me you don't care if your wife is sleeping with another man, there just isn't any option."

I let my hands fall to the table with a dull thud. "I want you to tell me I'm crazy, that I must have imagined it, that there's no way in the world Claire would do such a thing."

Mother sighed. "Sweetheart, I wish I could tell you that, but the truth is that sometimes people are capable of things that take you by surprise."

I heard a tapping sound beneath me and looked down to find it was my own feet bouncing on the hardwood floors. "I just wish I knew for sure," I said.

"Confronting her is the only way to know for sure," my mother said. "It's not like you're going to hire a private detective."

I heard my feet stop.

"Listen, Jonathan," she said, her voice lower, "you're a grown man, you can make your own decisions. But don't do anything crazy."

I nodded, and she looked a little relieved. Which suggested she'd interpreted my nod to mean I wouldn't do anything crazy. But that wasn't the way I meant it at all.

WHEN I ARRIVED AT the office I went directly to see Bruce. I found him with his leg on the desk, icing his calf. "Getting old is a bitch," he said without looking up. "But it won't stop me from kicking your ass again today."

I sat down and stared past him out the window toward the towering skyscrapers of midtown. "Bruce, can I ask you something?"

"Yeah."

"It's not an easy question."

"What is it, man?"

He is very direct, Bruce. It is his best quality.

"I want to ask about your marriage," I said.

Bruce's eyes narrowed in a little smile. "This should be interesting."

"I find myself wondering . . . about . . . your *arrangement*. You know. The city?"

Bruce scratched his chin. "I'm a pretty smart guy, but for the life of me I can't think of why you would be asking me such a personal question."

I desperately didn't want to get into details. "Something happened," I said uneasily.

"You all right, Johnny?"

"I'm fine. But . . . I have concerns about my marriage. I need a little guidance."

"Okay," Bruce said, stretching out his leg. "I'll say this: What works for Helen and me may not work for everyone. It doesn't have to work for anyone else. It just has to work for us. It's all about boundaries. I do what I do, but never at home and never with anyone that could connect to us."

"So, you're discreet?"

"That's a bullshit word, Johnny. I do what I do and I make sure it never winds up in her face. If it does, she takes me for half of everything."

I nodded, took a deep breath. "Bruce," I said even more tentatively. "Do you remember that time with Fernandez?" He nodded. "I need some help of that kind."

Bruce leaned closer immediately. "I'm going to give you an address right now. I am not going to write it down, I just want you to remember it." He told me the address. "He'll be expecting you in one hour."

REGGIE FERNANDEZ HAD BEEN an executive at our firm who departed for a competitor and, we suspected, violated terms of his contract by copying files and other sensitive data before giving his notice. Fernandez worked on my team, so it was me to whom he quit.

"Fernandez is going across the street," I had told Bruce. "And between you and me, I don't have a good feeling about protocol."

Bruce nodded. An angry look flashed across his face but only for a moment, then he leaned back in his leather chair. "Disappointing," he said. "Seemed like a decent kid."

"He's smart. And ambitious. Sky-high."

"Not surprised then," he said. "That young, they think they're invincible."

"How do we handle?"

"Is he married?"

A chill went up my spine. "Yes, he's married," I said.

Bruce picked up his phone. "I'll take it from here. See you on the basketball court in an hour."

I hadn't thought much about that conversation since. In part because it was the only one of its kind we ever had, but also because it rather scared me, like something out of a John Grisham novel. A week later I heard that Fernandez had made a startling decision: he turned down the offer from our competitor and was instead moving his family out west to work for a smaller firm. It was the talk of our office for several days but I never asked any questions. As my mother said, sometimes it's hard to imagine what people are capable of.

I'M NOT SURE EXACTLY what I expected a private detective to look like.

I guess I pictured Peter Falk, crumpled and quirky but trustworthy. Lowell Cranston didn't look anything like Columbo. He was tall and thin, probably six foot five, with neatly parted hair and a well-kempt mustache. He wore a tight-fitting gray suit and slim black tie, more European banker than private eye. His office was small but tasteful, furnished more like a living room than a place of business: mahogany desk, bare hardwood floors, leather sofa, flat-screen television, fully stocked bar.

"Welcome," Cranston said with a warm smile, rising from behind the desk as I entered. "Can I get you a drink?"

"Tempting, but no thanks." I sat on the couch.

"If you feel ill at ease, Mr. Sweetwater, let me assure you that is very much the norm. Most of my clientele is of the sort that never imagined they would be sitting with a private detective. You're thinking you need to explain to me that you are a normal, upstanding family man, a pillar of society. You needn't bother. I know who you are."

I nodded. And regretted not accepting the drink.

"Let me tell you a few things," Cranston went on. "You'll notice there was no one at the door to greet you, no assistant, no secretary, no partner, no intern. In this office, and in our transaction, you will deal with me and me alone, and I am the only one who will ever be aware this meeting took place. If we decide to proceed together I will remain the only person alive who will ever know of our dealings. In short: your secrets are safe with me. So why don't you fix yourself that drink you're reconsidering, make yourself comfortable, and let's figure out what's going on."

In the refrigerator I found a tray of freshly sliced limes, each covered in thin plastic wrap. I took two and peeled the protective layer off each, squeezed one into a glass, and dropped the other in whole. Then I unscrewed the cap from a bottle of tonic water, filled a third of the glass, sloshed it about so the lime juice disappeared into the bubbles, then topped it with Grey Goose. "I don't really know where to begin," I said, still facing away. "What did Bruce tell you?"

"Mr. Sweetwater, I cannot confirm that I am acquainted with anyone named Bruce, just as I will never confirm to anyone that I am acquainted with you. As for the details of your case, I know absolutely nothing except what you will choose to tell me right now."

I turned to face him. "I think my wife is having an affair."

Cranston leaned back in his chair, hands clasped behind his head. He didn't say a word.

"Did you hear me?" I asked.

"I most certainly did," he said. "And I'm still listening."

I told him everything there was to tell. He took notes by hand without looking down. When I was finished I downed more of the drink in large gulps. It wasn't making me as drunk as I wanted to be.

"Nothing can change the world," Cranston said, "but we can change the circumstances. In my experience, the only way to do that is first to know precisely what the circumstances are. So, that is where we will begin. We must find out for certain that which you strongly suspect. Does that sound agreeable to you?"

"It does."

"That should not be complicated," Cranston said. "Do you have photos of your wife on your phone?"

"Not . . . interesting ones."

Cranston smiled. "I wouldn't expect that," he said. "I just mean regular pictures. It will make it easier for me to do this job if I know what she looks like."

I felt color rushing to my cheeks.

"You needn't be embarrassed," Cranston said. "I know what you're going through. You're thinking you are a successful, grounded family man. You have perfect credit, no police record, you've never been involved in anything like this in your life. Now you're sitting in the office of a stranger, asking him to shadow your wife. It is crucial for you that I know this isn't how you view yourself. And what I'm saying to you is that I understand. So, if you have any pictures let me see them and we'll get on with this."

I took another sip of the vodka and took my phone out of my breast pocket. "I don't have any," I said, "except this one." I showed him the screensaver, the four of us in face paint at Disney World.

"Nice family," he said sincerely. "If you provide me with your address and a few other details I can make do without the photo."

I looked up at the ceiling. There was a fan oscillating slowly, not enough to create any noticeable breeze. That was how I felt, like I didn't have enough energy to create a breeze.

"Phase one of this investigation should not take long," Cranston said. "You will soon receive an e-mail from 'Cranston and Associates.' It will be addressed to your first and last name, as are most solicitations. It will describe a series of insurance options that my firm would be happy to go over with you anytime at your convenience. When you receive the e-mail you will hit *reply* and type in a single digit, to correspond to the hour of the afternoon you wish to come here and retrieve the information. Do not bother typing P or P.M.; we have established now that the time will be P.M. So if you type a three, we will meet at three P.M. One digit only, because that is most easily explained as an accidental slip. I will meet you here on the day you send the reply at the hour you have indicated. Does all of this make sense to you?"

I nodded.

"Okay. You will hear from me shortly. In the interim, do not tell anyone of our meeting, do not look for me or try to contact me in any way."

"What if I want to call it off?"

Cranston looked at me sternly. "Then tell me that right now."

Of course I wanted to call it off. But I needed to know.

"Mr. Sweetwater, take all the time you need. If you want to call this off just say the word and you will never hear my name again. But if you walk out of this office with our arrangement in place, be aware that you are setting in motion a series of events you will not be able to fully control. There are certain sights in life that, once they have been seen, can never be unseen. Do you understand what I mean?"

"I think so," I said.

"I mean that once you know something you can do with it anything you wish, but you can never unknow it. And sometimes the things we do *not* know are better for us than those that we do."

"I understand," I said.

Though I didn't, really.

BRUCE AND I PLAYED basketball late in the afternoon. "My calf is seventy percent," he told me, "which is enough to kick one hundred percent of your ass."

As we headed to the gym I sent a note to Claire. *Bruce and I headed into the room now.* The words were truthful, even if they weren't honest. But what did it matter? I had already lied to her in the morning; that is the sort of thing that matters a lot less the second time.

I don't know that I've ever played worse than I did in that game. I was meek, subdued, lethargic, my heart beating so fast that within a few minutes I needed a break.

"You all right?" Bruce asked. He wasn't even sweating yet.

I was doubled over, hands on my knees. "Fine," I said. "It's just been a long week."

Bruce smiled. "I know just what you need."

I stood straight up, poked the ball from his hands. "What I *need* is to run your old ass up and down this floor, that's what I need." We picked it up again and I played better, though not much.

After a shower we were in the back of Bruce's limousine, and I felt like it was the first day of school: I was neatly scrubbed and combed, in my best clothes, going to a strange place to meet strange people. Bruce was fiddling with the channels on the television in the console, cursing the satellite service. "You pay four thousand bucks to have this installed and it *never* works." He was speaking aloud but not to me, which was fine because I wasn't really listening. "What's way better is *this*," Bruce said, pulling his iPad from his briefcase, "and it cost next to nothing. Slingbox. I watch whatever I want, wherever I want, so long as I get a signal."

I found the static from the television soothing, like the constant roar of the ocean. I was just going through the motions anyway. What I wanted was to be home, having dinner with my family. I wanted Claire to pour me a glass of wine while the kids put on a sketch they had been practicing all day, and then have the four of us sit down and Claire and I drink wine and the kids drink milk, and we'd be having salmon with broccoli, which both kids drown in soy sauce, and then chocolate chip cookies only for those who finish their broccoli. Drew is very particular about that rule; he makes sure there is not a speck of green on anyone's plate before they may have a cookie. His sister is the opposite: I've seen her fake the broccoli. If I wasn't going to be *there* it didn't much matter where I was. So the car seemed fine and the static on the television didn't bother me, and whatever Bruce wanted to talk about was no more or less interesting than anything else.

Our first stop was Nobu, the legendary Japanese restaurant on Hudson Street, where Bruce was welcomed as a celebrity. The greeter at the door, the hostess behind the desk, the waiter who took our drink order, and the manager who stopped at our table all called him by his first name, like they were old friends from college despite the fact they were young enough to be his children. We ate yellowtail sashimi, Japanese eggplant, and broiled Alaskan cod, drank beer and a little bit of wine. The air was light and electric, with the whiff of gourmet cooking and expensive perfume mixed with sex.

I was intent on paying the bill but that wasn't possible since no bill ever came. When we were finished, with a group of women hovering near enough to pounce, Bruce finished a final beer and turned to me, red in the face. "Ready to go?"

"We haven't paid," I said.

"Yes, we have."

"I never saw anything."

"That doesn't mean we haven't done anything," Bruce said.

I looked him in the eye. "I was going to take care of dinner."

Bruce smiled, his cheeks red with excitement, his eyes alternating between meeting my gaze and scanning the cluster eagerly encircling us. "Listen," he said, "that's a nice gesture, but what purpose could it serve?" He put his hand on my shoulder. "You're doing great. Everybody in this room would trade seats with you in a minute right now, except for me. And that's the way it should be. So let me pay. And someday, when you're sitting in *this* seat, you pay for whoever is lucky enough to be next to you."

I felt the hair on the back of my neck stand up.

"Do you feel lucky?" he asked.

I looked around. "It'd be pretty hard to feel any other way."

"Perfect," Bruce said, "let's go see how lucky we really are."

WHEN WE GOT TO the car four people were waiting. One of them was a man who appeared in every way out of place: notably older, probably seventy, with white hair and a neatly trimmed white beard, dressed impeccably in a tuxedo and bowler. His presence was curious, but the curiosity lasted only as long as it took for the three women to pile in behind him, dressed to kill, a dizzying array of hair and perfume. The older man did not say a word, but the women were all friendly; one of them goosed me as I slid around to an unoccupied seat. "Champagne?" She giggled, along with the other two.

Then we were rolling and drinking and Bruce was singing, at first alone but soon everyone joined him, including me, singing even though I couldn't hear the music. Eventually we pulled up in a darkened alley uptown and two cars pulled in behind us, headlights blaring; only then did I realize we had been leading a caravan. A dozen people spilled from the cars, looking exactly as we did, drunk and sensational, the women dripping with diamonds, teetering precariously on towering heels.

There was a sharp, intense popping sound right behind me, like someone had fired a very small gun, and I spun to find one of the younger and sexier women had popped the cork on a bottle of champagne with her teeth. The crowd cheered as she pulled back her lips and displayed the prize, holding aloft the bottle, a bit of the bubbly spilling onto her hand. I was the nearest to her, and she quickly jammed her face into mine as though she was going to kiss me, but instead forced the cork into my mouth. Then she took a swig directly out of the bottle and held it up again. "How do you like that, boy?!" she cried. Her eyes were crazy, wide and shining. With no warning, she snatched the cork from between my lips with her free hand, took another swig from the bottle, and then passed it to me. The rest of the group was still buzzing as I took a swig and passed it along, and when I turned back the woman was wiping her mouth with the palm of her hand and coming toward me again. Once more she jammed her lips into mine, only this time there was nothing between them but her tongue.

Then a door burst open right from the center of the bricks and a greasy fellow in a leather jacket and baseball cap came out. "You all with Bruce?" he asked.

Bruce emerged from the rear of our pack. "Eddie," he said, and raised his hand.

The greasy fellow nodded and, without another word, started counting us.

"Fourteen," Bruce said.

The guy nodded once more, then motioned for us to follow and went back inside.

THE ROOM WASN'T NOISY at all. The rhythm of the music and thumping of the beat provided ambience but they didn't drown out conversation; no one had to shout in order to be heard. That was the first thing I noticed. The next was the decor, surprisingly grown-up, like an old-time bar you'd find in an elegant hotel: wood, red leather, velvet, spacious booths in a ring around small wooden tables. All of the booths had been set aside for our group. Bruce slid into the first and motioned for me to slide beside him. "Not bad, huh?" he asked.

"Outstanding," I said. I chose that word because it is one Claire uses often, and certainly how she would have described this. Claire detests having to shout to be heard. She'd have been even more delighted than I was to be carrying on this conversation in a normal tone of voice.

The music and thumping bass were coming from another room. I looked around but couldn't find it. "Through that door," Bruce said, pointing past the bar. "Dancing all night. In here, we just hang out."

"Do we dance?"

"I have no idea what *you* do," he said with a smile, "but I dance my ass off."

Bruce motioned for our server, a stunning woman in a black blouse unbuttoned halfway, breasts bursting from within. "Table service?" she asked.

"Yes, Belvedere," Bruce replied. "And champagne."

The waitress then glanced at me, eyebrows raised. "Champagne and Belvedere for you as well, Mr. Sweetwater?" she asked.

"That sounds good," I said, my voice deeper than usual in my ears.

She pursed her lips and blew a strand of hair away from her face, and I followed her with my eyes until she disappeared behind a door. Then there was a hand on my leg, and the blonde who had popped the champagne with her teeth was close enough that I could feel every part of her: bare leg against my knee, bare shoulder against my arm, hand firmly on my thigh. Claire often rested her hand on my thigh but gently, her fingers at rest, light enough that you could forget they were there. This woman you wouldn't forget. I looked down at the hand, so different from Claire's: nails long, French manicure. Claire's nails are short. These were like talons. I could feel them digging into my leg.

When I looked up her face was startlingly close. "Do you want any blow?" she asked. Her eyes were clear and blue and danced in the flashing lights; frankly she was gorgeous, more so than I had realized in the car. Her hair was pulled back off her face and perfectly straight, her makeup more subtle than I would have expected, a dash here and there, fresh and young, not at all tawdry. And her lips were a masterpiece. There is nothing sexier than a great pair of lips. These were the best I had ever seen.

"I'm sorry?" I asked.

"Some of the girls have blow. I didn't know if you were into that." Her voice wasn't at all as I remembered it. Outside she had seemed wild, like an animal escaped from the zoo. Now her voice was more measured, the disaffected monotone of the teenage girls who babysit my kids on Saturday nights.

"Bolivian Marching Powder," I said.

She blinked.

"You know," I said, "from *Bright Lights, Big City.*"

"Right," she said. It was clear we should just move on.

"Are you from New York?" I asked.

"New Orleans."

"Great city."

She smiled and squeezed my leg harder. "I'm a Southern girl. People tell me my accent sounds like I'm from Brooklyn."

"How long have you been in New York?"

"Almost a year," she said. "I don't care for coke either, but I wanted to make sure you didn't miss out before the girls go off."

"I'm good."

"Me too."

We fixed ourselves drinks. It was then I realized Bruce had gotten up to dance; I hadn't noticed his leaving.

"Do you like to dance?" she asked.

"Do you?"

"I *love* it!"

"Let me have this drink," I said, "and then we'll see what kind of moves you've got."

WE DEPARTED THE NIGHTCLUB just after eleven o'clock. As Bruce always told me, partying into the wee hours is for movie stars and musicians who don't have responsibilities in the morning and want their pictures in the newspaper. "That's why most of them disappear so quickly from the spotlight," he would say. "How productive can anyone be if they're in nightclubs at two in the morning?"

Three limousines stood outside: two were going to Bruce's apartment, the third was for members of the group who didn't warrant that invitation. That driver was instructed to take each guest wherever he or she wished to go, one at a time, in whatever order made the most geographic sense. All of them embraced Bruce and me upon their departure, hearty hugs and handshakes, kisses on both cheeks. Then Bruce stepped into the first limousine and I into the second. My blonde slid beside me, sought out my hand, and held it with our fingers interlocked. There were four of us in the car. The three women immediately started gabbing about how delightful the club had been, how sparkling the glassware, how attentive the service, how perfect the music.

"And of course," my girl said, raising my hand, "*this* one here was the *best* dancer."

"It *was* spectacular to watch."

"I had no idea you had such *moves*."

"Bruce is *soooo* much fun."

"Oh, I just *adooooore* Bruce."

I took a deep breath and looked out the window. We were traveling through Central Park. The lights in the trees cast a staggered illumination, providing the very particular calmness that only comes from being in New York but feeling a million miles away. We all sat in silence, luxuriating in that moment of quietude that life so infrequently provides amid the madness.

There was a vibration in my chest, brief and gentle. I thought for a moment it was the excitement but just as quickly realized it was coming from my pocket. I went in discreetly with my free hand as though I were committing a crime, which I suppose I was. In this car there was no place for the intrusion of reality.

It was a missed call from Claire. I stared at the face of the phone and felt it vibrate again, this time in my hand.

> Hope you're getting a good sleep! I e-mailed pictures from the party! Miss and love! Xoxo

I breathed in deeply, let it out, then tucked the phone back into my pocket. No one in the group had paid any attention to my brief interlude with the outside world; they were too consumed with being fabulous.

We came out of the park and drove down Fifth Avenue: awnings stretched above austere glass doorways, uniformed doormen chatting, a well-dressed couple laughing, a cabbie having a smoke, a lady in a red coat walking a dog so small it could have been a hamster. A city at night, radiant and diverse and alive. I looked down at my hand, the fingers still thoughtlessly interlocking with the blonde's. Claire's hand was so small, this hand so different. Life is much simpler when everything is the same.

THE APARTMENT, WHICH I had seen but not in some time, was huge and luxurious: three bedrooms with walk-in closets, three baths with Jacuzzi tubs, designer furniture, granite countertops, giant LED televisions. When my blonde and I walked in there was soft music playing:

Al Green, Marvin Gaye. A pair of high heels had been strewn thoughtlessly on the carpet.

Bruce and his brunette were seated in the center of the sofa in the living room, both holding drinks, her bare toes digging into the plush carpeting. Behind them, around the kitchen island, were two other women and the white-haired man in his tuxedo, bowler still perched atop his head. They were mixing drinks and tapping rapid beats onto the counter.

Taptaptap. Taptaptap.

My blonde touched my arm. "Drink, Johnny?" she asked.

I nodded and she went to the bar. The taptaptapping model raised her eyes. "Want a line, Shell?" My blonde—Shell?—responded with a quick, firm shake of the head. It wasn't cool because I wasn't into it.

That emboldened me. "I may change my mind," I said, stepping toward them, "if I'm invited." I didn't have any intention of doing cocaine with these girls, but somehow I liked their having the idea that I might.

The taptaptapping brunette stopped tapping, looked over at me, smiled with exactly the sort of surprise I had desired. She was chewing gum, which is about the least appealing thing a woman can do, but nothing could detract from this woman's appearance. She was the opposite of my blonde: dark in every way, straight black hair, olive complexion. "Of coooourse," she said, resuming her tapping.

The model seated beside her was a mix of the first two, chestnut hair, athletic, like a tomboy someone had convinced to try the clothes and the makeup. Then she spoke. "This is heavy-duty shit."

Looks can be deceiving. The voice was pure disenfranchised model: cocaine, eating disorder, mean girl.

"It's been a long time," I said, "like twenty years."

"Yeah?"

"Len Bias changed my life," I said.

Nothing.

The dark-haired girl stopped the tapping and laid her razor blade on the countertop. There was a tiny mountain of white powder on a black sheet of paper, with six lines carved thin and a tightly rolled hundred-dollar bill wrapped in clear tape. "All yours," she said. The accent sounded French.

"Maybe in a little bit," I said. "I'd like a drink first."

The French brunette lifted her eyebrows a smidge, which could have meant "Suit yourself" or "I knew you didn't have the guts." I wasn't sure which, and I didn't care. The time in my life when impressing a girl like this would have been of paramount importance had ended the instant I realized I could have had any of the girls at this party. Disinterested models become a lot less alluring when they are interested.

My blonde poured me a drink. I took a swig and let it lay on my tongue.

"Did I get it right?" she asked.

"Perfect."

From behind us came a rousing snort, followed by a series of sniffles, then another snort. I turned, drink at my lips. The French girl, her face flushed, was rubbing her nose with the heel of her hand. A faraway look was in her eyes, but within a moment she looked normal again; made me wonder how many lines into the night she was. She held the straw out for me, tucked between her thumb and forefinger like a tiny cigarette, but I walked right past her into the living room. The music was still going but now the sofa was empty, and the door to Bruce's bedroom was closed.

A voice came from behind me, directly in my ear. "I haven't taken a *bath* since I've been in New York." Shell had followed me, practically in my stride. Now she was whispering loudly enough that I was pretty sure everyone could hear. "I'm going to try that Jacuzzi," she said.

Drink in hand, she slipped by, brushing against my chest so that my tie slid all the way to my shoulder. She walked slowly across to a bedroom and disappeared inside. The music was still playing: Dusty Springfield, "Son of a Preacher Man." I took a sip of my drink, pulled my necktie back into place, turned to see the girls at the counter tidying up. The mound of powder had disappeared, the lines too, all tucked away into whatever it is models keep their cocaine in these days. The tomboy was applying lip gloss, the French girl was digging a fresh piece of gum from her bag. Both of them stepped back into their heels, gave me kisses on both cheeks.

I raised the glass again and tilted my head all the way back, let every last drop slide between my lips. I was not thinking of Claire, or of my beautiful children, tucked into their beds an hour away. I wasn't thinking of anything at all. I simply put my empty glass down on the counter where the cocaine had been, and then, with great determination, walked through the open door toward the sound of the running water.

There was a trail of clothes leading to the bathroom. I bent to pick up a high-heeled shoe, turned it over—red sole—picked up the other and placed them both on a narrow table in the hall. Her dress was a few steps beyond, golden glitter, sparkling in the dim glow of a lamp. I picked that up, too, and laid it on the table beside the shoes. All that remained was a balled-up black thong, dropped carelessly at the spot where the carpet met the bathroom tile. I left that where it was.

I rounded the corner to find her in the tub, submerged to the neck. She wasn't as long as I'd imagined but she was stunning nonetheless, lean and tanned and muscular.

"How's the bath?" I asked.

"Better than I remembered. Why don't you join me?"

I stayed where I was, ten feet away, tie loose about my neck, sleeves rolled to the elbows. "Is your name Shell?"

"Shelby. My mom named me after the Julia Roberts character in *Steel Magnolias*. She was carrying me when she saw that movie. It's still her favorite to this day."

"I like the name."

"I like it too."

I went to the tub and sat on the edge, felt the seat of my pants dampen from the hot water. Shelby leaned forward until her face was beside mine. Her breasts were perfectly tanned and dripping wet, just a hint of bubble bath on her shoulders and chest. She threw her head back and gave me the length of her neck, which I kissed gently and then, tentatively, reached with my fingers until they found the tip of her breast. The instant my hand cupped her flesh she attacked me with her lips, kissing me so hard it was hardly kissing at all. Claire *never* kisses with her tongue. Claire's breasts are bigger, too, than these, which were perky and hard but hardly a handful.

Shelby rose to her knees and yanked hard on my collar, pulling me into the tub, fully dressed. I felt the heat and the rush and I couldn't quite breathe; Shelby was tearing wildly at the buttons on my shirt. As she began kissing her way down my chest I closed my eyes. Suddenly, I couldn't stop thinking of a different woman. Not my wife.

I met Melanie Koff my freshman year of college. She had ring-lets, dark eyes, and a voluptuous figure with which I desperately wanted to become acquainted. Our first date was dinner, our second a sorority party. Our third date, I was sure, was going to be the night. I arranged for my roommate to sleep elsewhere, dabbed on cologne, even wore my lucky shoes. Doc Marten loafers. Still have them in my closet.

I picked Melanie up and we went to dinner, then I took her to a movie she desperately wanted to see, a weepy Southern drama with a cast of famous women: *Steel Magnolias*. I didn't love it. Melanie, mean-while, began to cry halfway through and did not stop until the follow-ing day. Any romantic notions I had were cast aside; she was inconsolable. As I recall she saw the movie three times that week and never went out with me again; she found my reaction to it—or lack thereof—unacceptable. Melanie loved that movie, just as Shelby's mother did.

Then my mind spun forward, from Melanie to Claire. I pictured her sleeping in our bedroom. And just a few feet away, in the closet, were my Doc Marten loafers. That was when I opened my eyes, and looked down at Shelby, who was undoing my belt, and I thought to myself: *I own shoes older than this woman.*

"I apologize," I said, grabbing Shelby's hands and pushing her away. "I can't do this."

I rose to my feet and stood above her, dripping, my feelings a toxic mixture of contempt and loathing and pity. Then I climbed from the tub and sloshed through the hallway into the third bedroom, where I locked the door behind me. I went to the bathroom, peeled off my wet clothes, and dropped them in a heap in the tub. Then I climbed into bed fully naked and pulled the covers over my head. I was more tired than I'd realized. The last thing I remember thinking, as I drifted off to sleep, was that I had passed up sex with two beautiful women that day, and now I was naked and exhausted and alone.

THURSDAY

I HAD COFFEE AND croissants tucked beneath my arm when Mother greeted me at her door for the second time in as many days. "Now I know you're *really* fucked up," she said, smiling warmly.

"Can't I just be excited to spend time with my mother?"

She yanked the paper bag from me. "Give me those and tell me what's going on, because as delightful as it is to see you these visits are making me anxious."

"I love you too, Mother."

"If you really love me you'll start bringing oatmeal. Your marital strife is going to make me big as a house." She locked all the locks and slid all the chains and set the alarm behind us, then I followed her into the kitchen. She had thrown a housecoat over her nightgown; her face still bore the red outline of a sleeping mask.

"Did I wake you?" I asked.

"I was up," she said, and took her first sip of coffee. "But not very."

I was struck by how old she looked. Youthful for her age, perhaps, but youthful for seventy isn't as young as she used to be.

After I had told her about my night she just stared at me, chewing slowly, swallowing deliberately. She took a sip of her latte, savored it, never removing her eyes from my face. Finally, after licking her lips, she told me what she thought. "This is a complete mess. You're behaving like a crazy person. And, by the way, you look like hell."

I was wearing the workout gear I always keep handy, but I knew that wasn't what she meant. She was staring at my face, not my clothes. "I know."

She took another bite of the croissant. "Have you been sleeping?"

"I slept pretty soundly. But you're right, I'm a mess."

"So," she said, "what are we going to do about all this?"

"I really don't know." I rattled my fingers on the tabletop. "What would Percy have done?"

Mother stared at me, two fingers over her lips. "You realize that is the third time you have mentioned your father this week?"

"I wasn't counting," I said defensively, though my heart wasn't in it.

"You know whose name you have not mentioned as many times?" she asked.

I just nodded. There was no need for either of us to say it.

Mother stared harder over her glasses. "What I think you need to decide for yourself, Johnny, is who you are trying to figure out. Your wife? Your father? Or yourself? You cannot live your whole life pretending your father didn't exist *and* be obsessed with him at the same time. You need to move past him in your own mind so you can begin to deal with what *really* matters in your life, which is your marriage."

Before I could respond the buzzer sounded. Mother rose and pressed the button on the intercom. "That'll be the cleaning lady," she said.

She went to the door and I remained at the table, finishing my croissant. She was right. I needed to figure myself out before I could confront Claire; perhaps that was why I hadn't been able to do it already. But to figure myself out I first needed to come to terms with my father. The trouble was, I had no idea how to do that. He was gone and he wasn't coming back. I felt hopeless and crestfallen as I finished the last of my latte, and received little comfort from the sounds of the locks being opened, the familiar clicks and clacks of my childhood.

BASKETBALL THAT DAY WAS no different than any other.

I had just sent an e-mail to Claire explaining that I had slept soundly and felt markedly better when Bruce ducked his head into my office. We met on the court as we always did, we played hard, he won. Nothing out of the ordinary. When we were finished we sat on the bench, drank water. I had almost forgotten the previous evening entirely until Bruce slapped me on the thigh with a sweaty palm. "You have a good time last night?"

"Oh, yeah. Thanks for everything."

He waved away the gratitude. "We'll do it again."

"Hope so." I took a long sip of the water. "You leaving town today?"

"Going to see Helen's family in North Carolina, her parents' fiftieth anniversary."

"Nice."

He wiped his forehead with a towel. "Yeah, it is."

I started toward the shower. "Have a good time."

"I will," Bruce said, sounding in every way as though he meant it.

Then I was back in my office, drumming my fingers on the desk, staring at the pictures of my children. Phoebe age two, in a bathing suit on a sunny day, eating a chocolate Popsicle that had melted all over her face. Drew age eleven months, first swimming lesson, on his back in the pool at the YMCA, kicking his feet while I held him. Phoebe on a pony, Drew in a magician's hat, the four of us at Disney World, Claire holding Phoebe in a tiny bundle the day we brought her home from the hospital. On the floor in the corner of the office was a plastic garbage bag with my wet clothes. I thought I would drop them off at a dry cleaner in the city rather than the one in Connecticut where Claire brings everything. I would pay in cash so there would be nothing to trace to me. Or should I risk even that? Perhaps the best course was to throw the whole bundle in the trash after cutting off the mono-grammed sleeves.

I shook my head, angry with myself for behaving as though I had committed the crime of the century. I hadn't even done anything. Rather, I had done something but I hadn't done everything, and when everything is offered and you don't take it that feels much the same as having done nothing. So I was racked with guilt over an act I had turned down. It was like Claire always says about French fries: she loves them but doesn't indulge, because while she is eating them all she is thinking is that she shouldn't, and as a consequence she is disregarding her diet and not even enjoying it. That was how I felt, only in the reverse: I hadn't allowed myself to take what was offered, presumably because I was concerned over feeling guilty, but now I was feeling guilty anyway. So what was the point of passing up the naked woman in the bathtub?

What I really should have been thinking about was my wife, and I knew it. I took my phone from the breast pocket of my jacket. The text Claire had sent the night before popped onto the screen.

> Hope you're getting a good sleep! I e-mailed pictures from the party! Miss and love! Xoxo

I scratched my chin. I had gone through every e-mail in my inbox that morning, as I did every morning. There had been no pictures from Claire. I opened my inbox again and scrolled quickly through everything I had received, everything I had deleted. None of it had been from Claire, no pictures, nothing. As I clicked out of the inbox I leaned back in my seat and shut my eyes.

I knew I should have been wondering exactly where Claire was right then. But I wasn't. Instead I was thinking of the only time I was ever in Washington with my father. I was eight years old. Mother dressed me in a blue suit. Percy tied a tie around his own neck, loosened it, slipped it over my head, and pulled the knot to just beneath my chin. His hands were smooth and smelled of lime aftershave. We sat together in the back of a limousine, his hand on my knee. The radio played the news headlines of the day. We made two stops. The first was at my father's office on Capitol Hill, where he introduced me to his secretary, Christine. She told me I was a handsome young man. Percy asked her: "Are we confirmed with POTUS?" She said we were. Then we were in the car again, driving across the city. We had to pass multiple layers of security to enter the White House. The guards all looked very serious until they saw my father. Outside the Oval Office a red-haired woman was talking softly on the phone. She smiled as we approached, held up a finger, and mouthed the words "Is that your son?" When she hung up the phone she pressed a button on her desk. A uniformed military man appeared from behind an open door. The red-haired woman asked him to show my father and me in, and she ruffled my hair as I passed by. I took a picture with President Carter. He and my father laughed easily together. When we left, the driver was waiting with the engine running. He drove us back to the apartment where my father lived when he wasn't in New York. Mother was waiting and we went for dinner in a fancy restaurant. I was still in my suit. Percy ordered steak, so I did too. It had begun to rain when we left the restaurant but Percy said no one ever died from a little rain so we walked back to the apartment. By the time we arrived my suit was soaked, and so was Percy's. But he didn't seem to mind and I didn't either. It was the last time I remember having dinner with my father.

I opened my eyes, and then my browser to Google. Slowly, I typed in two words. *Sweetwater personal.* I had read it a million times before. It had always seemed like all I needed to know. Now I wasn't so sure.

There was a time the Sweetwaters were among the wealthiest families in upstate New York. The family ancestry could be traced to Jacques Claude Laidet, a French physiocrat, who emigrated to the United States during the French Revolution. He settled outside New York, where he married the scion of a wealthy manufacturing family, Edith Waters. The family assumed the name of Sweetwater and settled in Rochester, where they made an even greater fortune in agriculture. Percival Sweetwater I, the grandson of Jacques and Edith, moved his family to Manhattan during the Second Industrial Revolution and founded a financial firm that grew into one of the most successful in early Wall Street history. By the time of his grandson's birth, the Sweetwater fortune was valued at over forty million dollars. The Great Depression staggered the Sweetwater family, but still, Percy inherited a sizable fortune and never wanted for money.

He began his career in politics while still in his twenties and was fond of saying: "It's a good thing I was born rich, because I've never worked a day in my life." Upon his death, Percy's estate was valued at fifty million dollars, of which he left most to his favorite charities. The remainder was distributed among his six wives, though details were never made public. He also left an unknown sum to his only son, Jonathan, who refused to attend the reading of the will and asked that his inheritance be donated to various charities of his mother's choosing.

That was, in brief, the story of my father's life and, in some ways, of mine as well. Now I was thinking perhaps I needed to know more. About both of us.

Back to Google, I again typed in two words. *Sweetwater decisions.* I knew what would come up. Everyone knows the quote. But I wanted to make sure I had it exactly right.

"A nation," said the majority leader, "is not a living being, nor is it a collection of beings. Rather, it is a collection of the billions of decisions that have been made in our history and all those

decisions that are to come. We, as a people, will leave only one mark on this planet long after our time, and that mark will be the sum total of all the decisions we make."

My father spoke those words while touting his voting record as a member of Congress, and that phrase *The sum total of the decisions we make* became his political calling card; his autobiography was titled *Percival Sweetwater III: The Decisions We Make.*

I opened the speaker on my phone and punched in my mother's number.

"Hello?"

"Mother, it's me."

"Good grief, Johnny, what is it now? Yvette vacuumed up all my incense again and I'm late for my shrink."

"Of all the books written about Percy," I asked, twirling a pencil between my forefinger and thumb, "which is the best?"

There was a long pause; if not for the vacuum I would have thought we'd been disconnected. Then she sighed. "Sweetheart, you aren't going to find your father in any of those books." There was melancholy in her tone. "They write about his career, the brilliant politician he was, his ability to make people comfortable in his presence. All of that is accurate but he was a good deal more complicated than he wanted the world to know. I'm afraid the time to know Percy has come and gone. You need to accept that and worry about the people who are still here."

"Did they interview you for the books?"

"One of them did, but I didn't tell him anything. Like I said, your father was too complicated for that. You can learn what the man did from books, but you can't learn who he was."

The next question was one we had assiduously avoided my entire life. "How about the others?"

"No," she said, "as far as I know they didn't interview any of them either. Most of those books are old; I think he was still only on the doctor at that point. Long before the model for sure."

My father's wives. Much like the man himself, I knew what they did but I didn't know who they were.

"Maybe I should talk to them," I said.

"Good luck with that, sweetheart. I don't even know where they are."

I let the pencil fall to the desk. "I think I know someone who can help with that."

I hung up the phone and took a long look at the photos of my family on the desk. When you spend your entire life running away from something it may not matter where you go, but even so you eventually get there. Right then, right there, I arrived. I dialed another number, heard it answered on the first ring. "Cranston and Associates, this is Lowell."

"Lowell, it's Jonathan Sweetwater. I know you told me not to reach out but this is not related to the matter we discussed in your office; this is different. I would still like you to continue with the previous matter, but now I have something else entirely to discuss, a little bit more complicated, but I believe it will be right up your alley."

There was a lengthy pause. I couldn't even hear him breathing. "Hello?" I said.

"Yes, I'm here." His voice was curt, dismissive. "I'm sorry, whom did you say this is again?"

"It's Jonathan Sweetwater."

"I'm sorry, I don't know anyone by that name. I would appreciate if you do not call this office again. Thank you very much."

And he hung up.

FORTY MINUTES LATER, WITH a light sweat dampening my shirt collar, I was staking out a detective in the lobby of his own building. I couldn't stand outside for the pouring rain so I pretended to use my mobile, pacing in circles inside the revolving door while rain-soaked businessmen shook out umbrellas on the clean white floors, leaving damp footprints and streaks of black and gray.

My thoughts were jumbled and mostly incoherent, but the one I kept coming back to was that now I had literally lost my mind. I should have been on the train back to Connecticut, to figure out my marriage and everything I truly valued. Instead, I was standing in the lobby of an office building hoping for a freak of happenstance.

A woman was smoking a cigarette directly outside, and every time the door revolved the whiff of smoke enveloped me. It was a filthy smell, made my aching head feel worse. I could see her lips moving between drags; she was talking to herself or to someone else in her mind. People who talk to themselves are either angry or crazy and she had to be angry; she was dressed too well to be crazy. Her fingers shook as they lifted the cigarette to her lips, and her entire life flashed before my eyes. Ditched by a man she loved deeply, perhaps this very day, and now she was rehearsing what she would say when she saw him. And I realized, as her trembling fingers went to her mouth again, that my father was right. This woman, like all of us, was the sum total of the decisions she had made. And what she was saying, in a voice so low even she could not hear, was all the things she wished she had said before. When people speak to themselves what they are really talking about is all the decisions they wish they could make over again. But they can't, of course. And neither can I. We are all the sum total of our decisions, and when we have chosen poorly there isn't anything more we can do about it than stand alone in the rain and complain.

"Mr. Sweetwater." I spun around. It was Cranston, in a tan raincoat over a dark suit, close enough I could shake his hand without extending my arm. "I thought it was you," he said softly. "I was trying to catch your attention from across the way. You seemed preoccupied."

"I was," I said. Finding Cranston had been my intention, yet the sight of him added to my anxiety. "I tried to call you."

"I told you not to," he said. "I did suspect it was you but I cannot be too careful. I promised you complete discretion and that is my personal guarantee. What can I do for you?"

"Can we go up to the office and talk?" I scratched my head. "This is going to require a little explaining."

MY SECOND VISIT TO Cranston's office felt markedly different from the first.

"Are we coming along on our other matter?" I asked as he executed a simple search at my behest.

"We are."

"Anything I should know?"

"With your permission," he replied, without removing his eyes from his computer screen, "I would prefer to complete the report before I present any portion of it. It has been my experience that partial information is the most dangerous kind."

"That's fine," I said. I wasn't sure I was ready to hear it anyway.

"It shouldn't be much longer," Cranston said. His fingers continued to fly across the keyboard; I'm not sure I'd ever seen anyone type so quickly. I smiled as I considered the difference between Cranston and Bruce. My CEO pounds a keyboard like it's a basketball; you can hear him typing from outside his office door. Cranston hardly seemed to disturb the keys as his fingers danced among them.

There was a whirring sound across the desk. Green lights illuminated a printer directly before me, and as it began to spit out sheets of paper Cranston pointed toward it. "Hot off the presses," he said.

I left the papers where they lay. It had taken Cranston all of ten minutes to find that from which I had spent my entire life hiding.

"Would you like me to put together a folder for you?" he asked. "You can go over these any time you want."

"I just need a minute," I said, my voice less sure than it had been.

He rose from his chair. "Take all the time you need," he said, his shoes echoing on the hardwood floor. "I'll be next door."

Each piece of paper that streamed from Cranston's printer had a name, a photo, and an address. He had asked if I needed more but I didn't think I did. Whatever more I needed I would find out myself.

I arranged the pages in chronological order and laid them facedown. I could feel my fingers shaking on the desk. With a deep breath I turned over the first page. The face was one I vaguely recognized:

the secretary who had once told me I was a handsome young man. I had seen her one other time as well, on the last day of my father's marriage to my mother. She looked older in this picture, but there wasn't any question it was the same woman.

IN THE CAR EN ROUTE to LaGuardia, as my driver cursed under his breath at a taxicab that nearly ran him off the Grand Central Parkway, I arranged a business dinner in Chicago. Then I texted Bruce. *Dinner in Chi with Deutsch and Kramer. Something about this deal doesn't pass the smell test. Will update asap.*

Within a minute my phone rang. "You want to play ball in the morning?"

I was confused. "With you?"

"No, I'm on my way to see Helen's family. But Friday mornings are special. I'm going to text you an address. Ask for Aaron when you get there. Michael usually arrives around nine."

There was no need for a last name. "I'll be there at quarter of," I said.

"I'll tell Aaron you're coming. Have fun."

I leaned back in my seat. With a tingle spreading slowly from my fingers, I texted Claire. *Dinner in Chicago tonight. Could get messy. Tell kids I may play basketball with Michael Jordan in the morning.*

Again, my phone rang within a minute. "Michael Jordan?"

I laughed. "Bruce knows a guy."

"That's very exciting," Claire said, "but I'm worried about you. How are you feeling?"

"Much better," I said. The lying made my pulse beat faster. "Good as new after a night's sleep. You were right about the hotel."

"Will you be home tomorrow?"

"Should be. By the way, I never got those pictures."

There was a little pause. It sounded as though Claire was momentarily distracted. "Honey," I said, "is everything all right?"

"Fine, just a little hectic, as usual."

"Okay," I said. "So, I didn't get the pictures."

"Well, I sent them," she said, faintly, as though she had turned her face away from the phone. "There's just a lot going on today. Call me later, miss and love."

"Miss and love," I said, as I heard her end of the phone go dead.

I TOUCHED DOWN IN Chicago in time to check into a hotel and shower before dinner at Gibsons. The clients and I drank martinis and ate steaks, and we talked about basketball and money, not in that order. The clients were principals in a real estate firm, and they talked too openly about a transaction they wanted us to fund. By the end of the night I understood the deal better than they did.

Before shutting the lights in my hotel room I typed a note to Bruce. *Dinner with Deutsch and Kramer tonight. No way in hell we do this with them, I'll explain later. Hoops tomorrow morning. I'll tell MJ you said hello.*

I had barely closed my eyes when I heard the iPhone reverberate. I picked it up off the nightstand. *Get physical with him. He doesn't like that, gets in his head.*

It was after midnight back home. "Less than a minute," I said aloud, and smiled. "Typical Bruce."

FRIDAY

THERE IS A PARTICULAR smell to a gym where basketball is being played that I love.

I'm not sure about other sports because I never played anything else, but I have played basketball all my life and always loved the smell. I don't know if it's the hardwood or whatever is used to clean it, or the way perspiration smells when it seeps into it, or if rubber soles on high-top sneakers emit a scent when they squeak, or if the ball gives off an aroma when it bounces, but whatever it is there is a smell in the gym that I have loved from my very first time.

I was a grade-schooler then. My parents had just split up. Mother moved me downtown, and what I missed most about the apartment we left behind was not my father, but rather the smell in the hallway. We lived on an upper floor; I don't recall which, but I do vividly recall the aroma of fresh dill. It's a very particular scent, and the moment the elevator doors opened you would smell it. When we moved away I always remembered it, and when I was lonely it was that smell that I missed.

Our apartment downtown had no such smell; the gym replaced the dill for me. My mother decided I should try a sport to alleviate my sadness and she chose basketball. I had never even seen a game, but the moment that scent reached my nostrils I knew I was home. I feel that way to this day, regardless of where in the world I am or what is happening around me. When I smell a basketball court I feel like I belong.

Hoops the Gym is a place where basketball legends are made. At any given time one might expect to find aspiring college players, current NBA stars, even the Great Jordan, whose name is spoken in the reverential tones Hemingway used to speak of bullfighters. It takes a lot of nerve for a forty-year-old banker to show up looking for a game, but I had the nerve.

I ate a hearty room service breakfast at six: eggs and bacon and two glasses of orange juice. Then I spent my usual hour responding to e-mails. I called home five minutes before the kids would leave for the bus.

Drew answered. "Did you play with Michael Jordan?"

"Not yet. Maybe this morning."

"Tell him I think he's cool."

"I will."

"Tell him about the poster in my room."

"I will."

"Okay. Phoebe doesn't want to talk to you."

He lives to irritate his sister. "Put her on the phone," I said.

A little rustling, then her voice. "Hi."

"Why didn't you want to talk to me?"

"Who said I didn't want to talk to you?"

"Your brother."

"*Andrew!*"

I smiled. "It doesn't matter. What's going to be the best thing about school today?"

She paused a moment. That is one of the great things about my daughter: there are no throwaway questions with her. If you ask, you get a thoughtful answer. "Probably lunch."

"Okay, sweetheart, have a wonderful day," I said, and she hung up.

Usually when I call home I speak to Claire as well, and it does my soul good to hear her voice, but at that moment I thought it might actually work in the reverse. A wave of sadness washed over me as I laid the phone down on the nightstand. The tray with empty dishes was on the foot of the bed, a bit of dried yolk streaking the plate beside a half-eaten piece of toast. The coffee had gone cold. I turned away from it all, looked out the window. A gray pall lay heavily upon the Chicago skyline, dreary and cold. April in Chicago often looks and feels like the dead of winter anywhere else. I closed the blinds and went to get dressed.

It was raining tiny, frozen drops when I got out of the cab and jogged into the gym, my heart pounding. There is a tiny bit of little kid in all of us, and Michael Jordan is the one who brings mine out. There isn't anyone I admire more. To see him in person, in his prime, was like watching Picasso paint, or Mozart play, or Olivier play Hamlet. To actually play with him was enough to make me forget why I was in Chicago in the first place.

I pulled open the door of Hoops and bounded up the stairs into the waiting area, where I found a tall man with shocking red hair and poor skin. "I was told to ask for Aaron," I said to him.

"I'm Aaron."

"Bruce Sellers sent me."

Aaron smiled, teeth a little too large for his mouth. "I'll get you a locker."

I hung my suit carefully, changed into workout gear, laced my high-tops tight enough that I felt my ankles throbbing. They were Air Jordans, of course. The only brand I've worn for twenty years.

Back out of the locker room, Aaron pointed the way to the gym.

"Let me ask," I said, casual as I could. "MJ coming this morning?"

"Not in town."

"I thought . . ." I didn't finish the sentence.

I could hear the sounds of a game going on, the squeaking of sneakers, the unmistakable shouting of spirited competition. Aaron and I just stared at each other.

"You still want to play?" he asked.

I sighed deeply. "Not really," I said. "I have important business today. I just thought it was a once-in-a-lifetime chance."

"Suit yourself," Aaron said, and started back toward the front desk. "Feel free to hang around as long as you want."

I stood quietly and watched him walk away. Then I watched a few minutes of the game being played. Eventually I would put my suit back on and head to 100 East Bellevue. But there wasn't any rush. I had waited thirty years for this. Ten more minutes wouldn't make much difference.

EAST BELLEVUE IS A quiet street in the heart of downtown Chicago, something of an oasis from the bustle of Rush Street. The steakhouse where I'd eaten the night before was on the corner. On a busy night that corner overflows with tourists and high-powered business diners, but late morning is vastly different; only a few window-shoppers were strolling about, most of the activity centered around a Starbucks. Farther up Bellevue were manicured gardens in front of small, elegant houses, mature trees lining the sidewalk. The whole street would have looked perfectly at home in suburban Connecticut.

A few steps from Lakeshore Drive I found the austere skyscraper, appropriately fashionable for its proximity to Michigan Avenue. There was a circular driveway in front of a glass revolving door, and a doorman behind a desk, thumbing through a newspaper.

I had envisioned standing outside, waiting however long it took, but now I saw a significant flaw in that strategy: it was unimaginably unpleasant outside. The freezing rain had ceased but the air was dank and cold and the wind coming off the lake tore through my suit. I loitered for as long as I could stand it, which was less than ten minutes, then I pushed through the revolving door into the lobby.

"Good afternoon," the doorman said, looking up from his paper. "How may I be of service on this gloomy day?" There was a cheerfulness about him that infuriated me for absolutely no reason.

"I'm here to see Christine Sweetwater," I said, my voice lifeless in my own ears.

"All right, sir," he replied, lifting an old-fashioned telephone from its cradle. "Who may I tell her is here?"

I didn't hesitate. "Her son, Jonathan."

The doorman didn't hesitate either. He opened a directory and scanned through with his forefinger, humming cheerily. "Just one moment, sir."

Obviously, he was new on the job. If his disposition wasn't enough to give that away, his search for her apartment surely did. In buildings such as these, veteran doormen knew the apartment numbers of their residents backward and forward. This fellow didn't know Christine well enough to know which unit she lived in, nor that she didn't have a son named Jonathan. But he was about to find out both.

"Yes, good afternoon," he said into the phone. "Is this Mrs. Sweetwater?" Brief pause. "Yes, your son is down here to see you." Longer pause. "Yes, I'm sure." He looked up at me curiously. "Are you Jonathan Sweetwater?"

I nodded.

"Yes, he is." Another pause, then the doorman hung up. He didn't look as cheerful anymore. "She says she'll be right down." I smiled as he went back to looking at his newspaper. Something in the exchange had lightened my mood. When you are feeling low, there is a perverse, unproductive pleasure in dragging others down with you.

It wasn't long before I heard an elevator door lurch open and I turned to find a face I had seen before, too long ago to remember. "Jonathan," Christine said, extending both hands. "My, look at you."

She was petite and pretty, in an overly made-up way. Her hair was cut medium length and straight, chestnut brown, parted on the side and spilling over the fur collar of her jacket. Her clothes were expensive but overdone, fancier than you would need for a ride in an elevator.

I took both her hands and shook them. "It certainly has been a long time."

I was a head taller than she, which only added to the awkwardness. We stood a moment holding hands, looking each other up and down as though we were preparing to try ourselves on. "What brings you to Chicago?" Christine asked at last.

"Business," I said. "I work on Wall Street. I had a dinner here last night. I had some time free today and have always thought about looking you up, so I thought I'd take a chance."

"How nice." Her smile appeared genuine. "How did you know where to find me?"

I was prepared for that. "My mother. She kept tabs on everybody all these years."

Christine's face clouded. "My goodness, she must hate me."

"She doesn't. My mother doesn't hate anyone. She let it go a long time ago."

"That's nice of you to say."

"I mean it. I wouldn't lie to you about that."

"Well, that's very nice," Christine said.

We were still holding hands. Two strangers distantly connected with nothing to say, nodding to fill the excruciating awkwardness.

"Can I buy you lunch?" I asked. "I wanted to talk to you."

"Of course. Where would you like to go?"

"It's your neighborhood; why don't you choose."

"Do you mind a little walk?"

I turned to look out through the glass. "It's a little cold."

Christine burst into a sharp laugh. "My, you are just like your father. He couldn't take the cold at all. Let me tell you, for Chicago *this* is not cold."

"Well, how far are we talking about?" I asked. It seemed pretty cold to me.

"My goodness, take my arm and let's go. A little suffering does a body good."

An icy chill burst through me, stopped me in my tracks. I dropped her hands. "What did you say?" I asked.

"A little suffering does a body good. Your father used to say that all the time."

THE WALK UP MICHIGAN Avenue was brisk but beautiful. When the wind wasn't roaring off the lake it wasn't too bad; I was able to appreciate the venerable, iconic architecture of the Magnificent Mile, the Drake Hotel, the John Hancock Center. When the breeze blew harder I tugged my collar around my neck and shivered. Christine cackled all the way at how cold I was; she hardly seemed to notice the wind. "I grew up in Des Plaines, a little town about thirty minutes north and west of the city," she said. "You get away from these tall buildings, that's when you really feel the wind."

"My father didn't like the cold?" I asked.

"Not at all. Only came to Chicago in the spring. 'No place in the world more beautiful in May,' he used to say. 'The trouble with Chicago is the other eleven months of the year.'" She changed her speech when she imitated him, not as much the voice as the cadence. It sounded familiar.

"What else did he used to say?"

She tugged my arm and pointed. "Here," she said. "This is where we're going for lunch. Let's get you warmed up and then I'll tell you anything you want to know about Percy."

ACROSS MICHIGAN AVENUE FROM the Hancock Center is the Bloomingdale's building, six floors of upscale shops and eateries amid the wonderful smell of luxury and opulence.

"This is beautiful," I said.

"It is my favorite place on a chilly day," she said, and smiled. She hadn't even bothered to zip her jacket. "Just coffee?" she asked. "Or are you hungry?"

"I'll eat lunch if you will."

"Perfect."

On the sixth floor was a restaurant called the Oak Tree: coffee bar and bakery in front, hostess station behind, restaurant with panoramic views of the skyline in the back. I frowned at the cluster of people milling about the hostess. "Crowded," I said skeptically.

Christine patted my hand. "Don't you worry." She led me directly through the crowd to a handsome young man in a vest and tie who was maintaining a pleasant disposition while people complained about how long they had been waiting. When he saw us, he smiled broadly. "Mrs. Sweetwater," he said. "How nice to see you."

"Hello, Gerald," Christine said. "I'd like you to meet someone. This is Jonathan. Technically, he's my stepson."

Gerald extended a hand. "Pleasure," he said. "Just wait here a minute." He disappeared into the kitchen, returned before the door finished swinging. "Will you meet Maria in the coffee bar?"

"Of course. Thanks." Christine yanked me by the arm and we pushed through the crowd again. By the bakery counter stood a gorgeous blonde holding menus.

"Nice to see you, Mrs. Sweetwater. Right this way." She led us through a back door into the kitchen, where the temperature rose at least twenty degrees. We exited through a door on the opposite side into the rear of the restaurant, where a table for two was waiting against the window.

"This is perfect," I said. "Thank you so much."

"Enjoy," said the blonde.

I held Christine's chair for her and then sat opposite, unrolling a yellow cloth napkin. "Nice to have connections," I said. "How did you manage that?"

"Tip well," she said. "And marry a senator."

CHRISTINE ORDERED THE CHEF'S salad. I had a ham and cheese omelet. We both drank iced tea. She sat with her back to the window, observing the room, leaving me the sensational view. No matter how gray the sky, there is something wonderful in the view of a big city at midday.

We made a great deal of pointless chat while we ate. She was waiting for me to start asking questions, and I suppose I was waiting for that too. Meanwhile, I enjoyed her company. Christine had a brazen quality, like a woman who'd spent a lot of time being judged and finally didn't give a damn anymore.

"So," she said after the dishes had been cleared and we were drinking coffee. "Tell me about your family."

"They are well, thank you."

"I'm glad to hear that," she said, stirring a third spoonful of sugar into her cup. "Who are they?"

I shook my head. "Of course. My wife is Claire. She grew up in New York, as I did. We live in suburban Connecticut now and have two children, a girl and a boy."

"How old is the girl?"

"She's nine. Going on nineteen."

Christine leaned back in her chair. "If I have one regret in my life it's that I never had a daughter. I think I would have made a wonderful mother to a girl."

"Did you have a son?"

"No, but that doesn't bother me nearly as much."

"Well, you would love Phoebe, she's a piece of work," I said.

"Phoebe," she said, running the name across her tongue like a taste of wine. "I love that name. Did you name her after the girl from *Friends*?"

"Actually, no. We named her after Holden's sister in *The Catcher in the Rye*."

"I always thought the one who played Phoebe on that show was the prettiest and the funniest but she seemed to get the least attention. I never understood that. So I'm glad you named your daughter after her. Even if you didn't."

I took a deep breath. "May I ask a few questions?"

"Are you paying for lunch?"

"I would be honored."

Christine smiled. "Then you can ask anything you want."

"Why did you and my father divorce?"

She shrugged. "He found someone else. Makes sense if you think about it. Our relationship began when he was married to someone else, so why would I have expected otherwise?"

"So you were involved in a relationship with my father when he was still married to my mother?" I'm not sure why I phrased that as a question. I knew the answer, and she knew I knew.

"I suppose I should apologize to you," she said, "but it seems well past the time for that. If I were to see your mother I would apologize to her. In fact I would like to, because if she felt anything like I did when it happened to me, then an apology is the least I could do."

"Do you mind if I ask how old you are?"

Christine didn't answer, nor even look in my direction. She just went on stirring her coffee.

"I'm sorry if that's an inappropriate question," I said.

"It is inappropriate and I wouldn't tell almost anyone else the answer," she said slowly, "but I *did* break up your parents' marriage so I guess I owe you one." She took a sip. "I'm sixty-one years old."

"So you're ten years younger than my mom."

"Almost exactly. I just had my birthday last week and if memory serves, your mother's is next week. Is that right?"

I nodded.

"Percy always used to say I was *exactly* ten years younger."

"How did he say that? Like bragging?"

Christine shook her head. "The opposite. The press gave Percy a hard time about my age. Remember, I was almost thirty years younger than he was. But he would counter by saying, 'She's only ten years younger than Alice, *that's* the number that counts.'"

It made me uneasy to hear her use my mother's name. "How did he get away with that?" I asked. "The press would destroy someone for that today."

"That's true, but things were different then. Plus, they loved your father."

"The press did?"

Christine leaned in over the table. "Jonathan, I assume you already know this, but *everyone* loved your father."

"I know that," I said. "I'm here because I'm trying to figure out why."

"It isn't easy to explain," Christine said, her eyes glancing upward, less toward the ceiling than toward the past. "He had enormous energy that was very magnetic; I never recall hearing him say he was tired. He was amazingly intelligent, as you must know; I never met a smarter man in all my life. And he knew everything. Go find another man who understands economic policy, orders wine in French, and plays Gershwin on the piano. I dare you."

Right then I knew the trip had been worthwhile. That was the best explanation of my father I had ever heard. "Can I ask you something else?" I said.

She nodded pleasantly.

"What happened at my ninth birthday party?"

Christine sighed heavily. "What do you remember about it?"

"I don't really remember anything except my mother shouting at Percy in front of everyone. It's the only time I remember her acting that way, even to this day. And I know I never saw my father again."

"And you have no idea why?"

"I have some idea," I said, "but I'm not clear on all of the details."

Christine paused. Then she said, "Okay, I guess I owe it to you. That day, Jonathan, was the biggest mistake your father ever made." She took a sip of coffee, stared right into my eyes. "As I'm sure you know, Percy famously said we are the sum total of the decisions we make. Well, he was right. And he was a brilliant man who made thousands of decisions in his life. The one he made that day was probably the worst. Your mother told him she never wanted to see him again and I couldn't blame her, and neither could Percy. He went away and stayed away, and he respected your desire not to have a relationship with him. So it cost him his son and it probably cost him something else that was even more important to him."

"What was that?"

Christine waved the question away. "Let me tell you what happened first, because I think it is important that you know he didn't mean to create the harm he did. Your father was a self-centered man, but he wasn't mean. There was no malicious intent on his part." She took another sip of the coffee, leaving a tiny smudge of red on the rim of the cup, which she wiped away with her thumb. "As you know, I was your father's personal secretary. It was a dream job for me. I was a girl from the suburbs of Chicago. I didn't have many skills but I had one that became legendary: I could type. In those days typing still mattered; in fact to be a secretary it was about all that mattered. And I was the best. The fastest you ever saw. I won competitions; I was the fastest and most accurate typist in the state of Illinois. When I finished high school I moved to the city and lived with my aunt on the northwest side, and I got a job at city hall as a secretary. Pretty quickly I moved up because my typing was so good, and within a year I was working directly for Mayor Daley. You probably know how close Daley was to your father; that was how I met Percy. Some of the girls in the office who knew him bragged about my typing. He told me he needed to see for himself. He was very charming and funny; he dictated a make-believe letter to the Kremlin with all sorts of threats and jokes and it had everybody howling. I was in love with him immediately, of course. And he was flirting, I could tell. That's how it began. Before I knew it, I was moving to Washington and working on Capitol Hill."

The restaurant had emptied around us. A light rain was falling again, the tiny drops streaking the windows.

"I knew he was married. Should that have stopped me? I guess it should. But I honestly believe any woman in my position would have done exactly what I did. Our relationship was in Washington, and only in Washington. I lived in his apartment in Georgetown and we barely made any effort to hide that. Your mother stayed in New York, so when he was there he was with her and when he was in Washington he was with me. I don't know exactly when your mother knew about us but she had to. She was no idiot, and like I said, we didn't make much effort to conceal it. I regret that part of it now; it had to be humiliating for your mother. But I was a kid and I was sleeping with one of the most powerful men in the world, so I wasn't thinking clearly."

The waiter approached the table but she shooed him off without looking in his direction. Her eyes never left mine. "This went on for years, Jonathan. Your mother hardly came to Washington in all the time I worked for Percy, and when he went home to New York I stayed behind. I only traveled with him when it was absolutely necessary, and when I did I stayed in a hotel away from the family."

"Until my birthday party."

"That's right." She sighed lightly. "Percy needed me on that trip because he was addressing the United Nations. He wrote all his own speeches, you know. He would write them by hand on a legal pad and then I would type them up for him; I knew exactly how he liked them. That was a big speech so he wanted to work on it right to the last minute. I was staying at the Waldorf, finishing up the speech, when he rang me from the front desk. It was pouring rain, he said, traffic was miserable. He had planned to go to your party and then pick me up on the way to the UN but with the traffic he was worried it wouldn't work, so he said to come down and we would stop at the party on the way. I didn't think much of it. All the way in the car we were going over the speech. We got to the place where the party was and he told me he would just be a few minutes."

"At my birthday party?"

"That's right. He went inside and I stayed in the car, and right away the driver said to me: 'I'm not feeling so well.' To this day, I don't know why he waited for your father to get out of the car to say that.

Then he started throwing up onto the empty seat next to him. It was unbearable; there was no way to stay in the car. It was a rainy day but I got out and stood on the sidewalk and waited. Then the driver put down his window and said to me: 'I radioed for another car, he'll be here in ten minutes.' And he drove away! The speech was in the back of the car! What was I going to do?"

I nodded. "So you went inside."

"I didn't have any choice. I tried to get Percy's attention without anyone seeing me, but that wasn't possible. He was completely surrounded by people, as usual. And before he saw me, your mother did."

I knew what happened next. "My mother told Percy she wanted a divorce, right there in front of all those people he was talking to."

"I couldn't blame her," Christine said. "It was her son's birthday party."

"Did they have an understanding?" I asked. "Did she accept it so long as he kept it away from her?"

"I honestly don't know. You'd have to ask her. That wasn't the sort of thing you talked about back then. Maybe it is now. In any event, by the time we got back outside the new car was there. It took us to the UN. Your father delivered his speech from memory and it was perfect."

I thought about that for a moment. "He got thrown out of his son's birthday party, his wife said she wanted a divorce . . ."

"And an hour later he delivered a speech to the entire world from memory as though nothing had happened. I told you he was amazing. I would never have wanted to play poker against your father, that's for sure."

The image of Claire in our driveway popped into my head. She was flipping through the mail, greeting me with no visible shock when I surprised her with the kids. For the second time, I felt a chill. "What happened after the speech?" I asked.

"We got back in the car to go to the airport. I was a wreck. But your father was very quiet. He would hardly talk at all. Finally, I asked him what was going through his mind. He said he was crushed, because the only dream he'd ever had in his life was to be president, and now there was no chance of that."

I put both hands to my face. My skin felt dry. "So, what you're telling me," I said, "is that after humiliating my mother at her son's birthday party, his primary concern was his political future."

Christine looked sad. "That is what I'm telling you, yes."

"Did he ever express any regret or concern about me?"

"Yes, he did."

"But his first thought was that now he'd never be president."

"Yes, it was. I'm sorry, Jonathan, but I don't see much point in lying to you about all this unless you want me to."

I shook my head.

"I didn't think so," she said. "He meant what he said that day, too. His turn in the party would have come next, but he decided not to run."

"Because of what happened with my mother?"

"I have always thought so. It would have been a scandal."

I leaned back in my chair. "I don't have any idea how to feel about this," I said. "I assume I should feel insulted and hurt, or at least sad. But mostly I just feel numb."

Christine looked at me with pity. "Your father was a complicated man. He never wanted to hurt anyone, but he didn't give much thought to anything except for how it affected him."

"As time went on, did he show much regret about me?"

She just patted my hand again, which I took as the answer to the question.

AFTER I PAID THE check we walked back to her building. The wind had died down so it was warmer, but not much. We didn't speak during the entire walk. I was trying to decide what I had learned, and I wasn't certain it was anything at all. I was wondering if I was like my father, in any way, and thinking I probably was not. Maybe Claire was. Maybe she was more like Percy than I would ever be.

When we arrived back at the revolving door I looked into Christine's eyes. "Can I ask one last question?"

"Of course."

"Why did the two of you split up?"

She snorted sarcastically. "He moved on," she said. "At first he told me I made him feel young. Then he met *her* and told me *she* made him feel young."

"So he wanted to feel young?"

"Maybe," she said. "I always thought it was an excuse, but I guess he might have meant it." Christine leaned in and gave me a light kiss on the cheek. "It was lovely meeting you," she said. "I enjoyed our conversation. You seem like a very nice young man. Whatever it is you're looking for, I hope you find it."

She went in through the revolving door and I watched her slowly walk away until she disappeared behind another door. It felt colder again, now that she'd gone. I tugged my collar up over my throat. Then the same doorman was standing beside me.

"Anything else I can help you with?" he asked.

"I need to get to O'Hare," I said.

He had a whistle on a string around his neck. He put it to his lips and blew two shrill blasts. I looked up the block and saw a Yellow cab pulling away from the curb and inching toward us. I took a twenty-dollar bill from my wallet and handed it to the doorman as the taxi came to a stop.

"Thanks, my friend," I said as he opened the door for me. "Keep on smiling."

IT WAS A SIGN, I thought, when my flight to LaGuardia was delayed and there was another to JFK a few gates away, and on the way I encountered one headed for Denver. Aspen was the next stop on my list, and suddenly the idea of going home first was the one that didn't seem sensible. It didn't matter that I hadn't any plans, or a ticket to board, or that my wife and my life were expecting me. I had discovered the magic of lying, like a drug, addictive if you let it be; so easy to be where you wished and do what you wished when you removed the shackles of truth.

I texted excuses to Claire (conference in Dallas) and Bruce (more clients in Chicago), then I rushed to the counter to beg the ill-informed attendant to please allow me to switch planes on account of an unspecified family emergency. She looked me up and down twice; I could see the wheels turning in her mind. *No way a guy in a suit this expensive is making up a story.* She switched my ticket without a word, even preserved my first-class status. I stared gratefully into her brown eyes. "Bless you," I said.

I had to kill three hours in the Denver airport before my flight to Aspen. I went to the lounge, sat in a quiet corner, drank coffee and watched my hands tremble. It was the lying that was getting to me. I'm not cut out for it. I kept imagining myself stricken in some way, hospitalized or killed, and Claire being informed, and before the first tears had rolled off her cheeks she was looking up in confusion and saying: "Wait, he was *where?*"

I put down the coffee, turned my palm toward me, and studied it closely. The zigzagging lines were deeper than they used to be. Turning the hand over I found my knuckles disobligingly red, the veins blue. The hands of an older man.

Get over it, I told myself. *You can't plan your life around what will happen if the plane crashes. And if it does, at that point it becomes someone else's problem.* The voice I was hearing belonged to my father. Whenever I gave myself a pep talk, it was his voice I heard.

In any event, the plane didn't crash. It landed bumpily just as night was falling in the mountains. The darkness spread slowly as I rode a taxi into town, where I took a room in the Hyatt Grand Aspen, at the base of Aspen Mountain. I had been to Aspen once before, as a boy, but remembered little more than the abject stillness. Now the serenity was palpable, in the air and the casual smiles on faces in the street. As a New Yorker it is my nature to distrust an unprovoked smile, the assumption being it must be born of insanity or ulterior motive, but in Aspen the smiles seemed to come easy.

I hung my suit in the closet, splashed water on my face, and ventured into the cool night, which smelled of freshly mown grass and a distant campfire. I strolled through town with no destination and no goal, stopping before nearly every storefront, admiring a leather saddle, a luxurious fur, a painting of a woman in a white dress on a beach. Two things occurred to me: that I was hungry, and that there aren't many things better in life than a walk when you don't have anywhere to go.

Above the bar in a restaurant called L'Osteria they were showing a basketball game, the Knicks in the playoffs. I ordered a bowl of pasta and a glass of white wine and watched the game. The people in the restaurant all seemed to know each other, but not in an exclusionary way; I was sure I would be welcome to join any group. I didn't wish to sit with any of them, content with my basketball, but it felt good to know that I could.

The altitude struck just as I was finishing a third beer. It was only nine o'clock local time but I felt as though I hadn't slept in a week. I left a generous tip and stumbled climbing down from the bar stool. I waved a friendly good night to the waiter and bartender and some of the diners who had shown me such imaginary hospitality. The fresh air perked me up, and I realized I hadn't once looked at my phone since I'd arrived.

Sixty-one e-mails, seemed about right. Just one text. *Getting into bed. Please message me when you get there safe and sound. Miss, miss, miss and love, love, love. C*

I took the deepest breath I could muster, taking inventory of all my organs. Nowhere inside could I find a place that felt guilty. A beautiful woman was writing me sweet words while I was atop a mountain a thousand miles from where she thought I'd be reading them, yet it triggered no emotion in me whatsoever. As I walked slowly back to the hotel, delighting in the night air, I wasn't sure if that constituted progress or a sure sign of the beginning of my demise.

SATURDAY

ALCOHOL AND ALTITUDE DO not mix. I slept hard but badly and awoke thirsty, head aching. It was just before six when I pulled open the blinds. When the sunlight flooded the room my aches instantly disappeared, replaced by a powerful surge of energy. The mountain just outside the window beckoned, lush and green. I stumbled out to the street in rumpled gym clothes, looking for breakfast. Behind the counter at Paradise Bakery I found a curvaceous young blonde, no more than twenty, with a warm smile and a steel rod embedded in her tongue. "Top of the morning!" she said. Her gleeful expression and youthful innocence stood in stark contrast to her piercing.

"That *must* have hurt," I said.

"It did," she replied, her eyes widening, "but it was soooo worth it."

Something inside me stirred. "I need coffee," I said, "badly."

"I only make it well," she said. "If you want it served badly you'll have to go somewhere else."

"What else do you serve well? I'm starving."

She glanced at the chalkboard above her head. "Everything is fresh," she said. "Egg and cheese on a bagel?"

"Sounds terrific."

She spun on her heel and disappeared into the rear, emerging a moment later with a bagel in one hand and a giant knife in the other. "You can come around back and help yourself to the coffee if you like," she said. "We don't open until seven."

I looked at my watch. "That's a half hour. I'm sorry if I'm causing you any trouble."

She stopped midslice and stared hard into my eyes. "Do I look troubled?"

"You do not."

"So, get some coffee."

I selected the largest of the three cups and filled it to the rim with black coffee, rich in color and texture. "This is wonderful," I said after a first sip. "It smells better than any coffee I can ever remember."

"It's the altitude," she said. "Everything smells better in the mountains. Where are you in from?"

"Is it that obvious I'm not local?"

She just laughed.

"New York," I said.

"Me too."

"Really?" I was surprised. "What part?"

"Upper west," she said. "Parents split when I was six, mom moved to New Rochelle. I couldn't wait to get out of there. I came out here the week after I graduated high school."

"How long ago was that?"

"Well, I'm legal, if that's what you mean," she said with mischievous eyes.

Behind her, the microwave issued a ding to announce the readiness of my eggs.

"It isn't," I said. "I swear."

"I don't believe you," she said. "But I'm nineteen, either way."

We stood in silence as she completed my sandwich and wrapped it in wax paper. I sipped the black coffee. Then she came from behind the counter to hand me my breakfast, staring directly into my face, and it was as though there was no air in the room, nothing separating us at all. I was sure if I took a single step toward her there would be no stopping us. I didn't, of course, because I am a married man and I don't do that sort of thing, even when naked supermodels are pulling me into a bathtub. I didn't with Shell and now I didn't again. But I thought about it this time, much more than I had thought about it before. "I didn't get your name," I said, coughing gently to clear my throat.

"Amanda."

"I'm Jon."

"Hi, Jon."

"Hi."

There was a pounding then, directly in my ears, and for a moment I thought it was inside my head but actually it was someone behind me, knocking on the glass. Amanda waved at whoever it was, and just like that the mood was broken. I dropped a twenty-dollar bill onto the counter and went to the door. "Thank you very much," I said. "Maybe I'll see you later."

"I'm here until two." She smiled sweetly this time, enough to make me wonder if I had imagined it all. But then I saw the rod in her tongue, and I was pretty sure I hadn't.

THE ADDRESS I HAD for Elizabeth was on Red Mountain, which the hotel told me was a lengthy walk, so I rented a bike. On the way, I was told, I would pass Smuggler Mountain, where many of the locals get their morning exercise: a jaunty, healthy climb, described by the concierge as "a heck of a lot better than spending a half hour on a treadmill."

"Amen to that," I said.

Surrounded by powder-coated Aspen trees and towering oaks, I pedaled out of town. My legs felt as though they could ride forever, but the altitude hit me square in the chest. I was gasping for air when I reached the base of Smuggler Mountain, where I left the bike unchained, leaning against a row of mailboxes. I unscrewed my first bottle of water and caught a second wind, then looked straight up the hiking path. It was jagged and rocky terrain, not the most scenic, but quite a workout in the bright sunshine. I wiped my mouth with the back of my hand and started up, choosing the steepest angle I could find, confident my chest would catch up with my legs.

The path was more crowded than I expected, with a wide cross-section of early risers getting their morning exercise: older women climbing slowly in baggy workout clothes, little dogs at their heels; younger women in athletic gear wearing earbuds and determined expressions; three muscular young men riding mountain bikes straight up, dripping sweat beneath helmets and sunglasses. One woman had twin girls on either side, the three of them holding hands, singing a distantly familiar song. I paused as I passed them, waiting for an ache that never came.

Then I began to run. It took me twenty minutes to reach the top, and to my delight, I found I was breathing steadily, with no hint of fatigue. A wooden sign indicated an observation platform, so I climbed through the bushes onto a dirt path. Just as I emerged into the sunlight, I felt my right sneaker sink into a slippery mass and slide; I caught myself just short of falling flat. I looked up to find a large dog and a small woman, with a face I recognized even though I had never seen it before.

"My goodness, Percy!"

I leaned back against a boulder and lifted my soiled sneaker into the air. "What did you call me?" I asked.

"I'm so sorry," the woman said, struggling to place a leash on a chocolate-brown Labrador more than half her size. "Percy," she said to the dog, "you naughty boy!"

Leaving my foot in the air, I reached into my backpack for the water bottle and took a long drink. I watched the woman and dog battle, with a familiarity on both sides that suggested this was a frequent occurrence. "Your dog is named Percy?" I asked.

"He is," she said without looking up. "And he is a *naughty boy.*"

"I thought I passed a sign that said dogs must be on leash."

"You did. I only let him off up here. But I turned my head for a moment and I can see what happened to your shoe. I'm awfully sorry." There wasn't any question it was Elizabeth; the flat, Midwestern accent clinched it. She was from Ohio, just outside Cincinnati, and you could hear it in the way she spoke. She looked just as I expected, not much above five feet tall, with auburn hair cut short and sparkling eyes. "I have paper towels in my pack," she was saying to me, having secured the dog. "Let me try to clean that off for you."

I took a good look at the shoe and thought it was a lost cause. "Good luck," I said.

"Don't give up so easily," she said, on her knees. "If you tell yourself you can't do something, you'll always be right."

A shudder went through me. "What did you say?" I asked.

She smiled and shook her head. "That's just an expression someone I knew used to use all the time," she said.

"Percy Sweetwater?"

She looked up at me, her eyes squinting in the bright sun. "How in the world did you guess that?"

"Your dog," I said. "Named Percy."

Now she had forgotten all about the shoe. She got up, dusted herself off and stretched to her fullest height, roughly to my chin. "You look familiar to me," she said. "Can't put my finger on it. Something in your face."

"I'm Jonathan Sweetwater," I said, and put my hand out to shake hers. "It's nice to finally meet you."

A smile broke slowly in the corners of her eyes, spreading to her lips. "Well, my goodness, Percy's son. I can't believe it, look at you. You look a little like your father," she said. "Not a lot, but a little."

In his autobiography, my father wrote that if he had ever started a company, this was the person he would have hired to manage it. He called her the most capable, organized person he had ever met.

"I'm Elizabeth Sweetwater," she said, smiling warmly, "and this has got to be the greatest coincidence of all time."

I smiled back. "No, it doesn't."

THE RESTAURANT WAS CALLED Ellina and the octopus was everything Elizabeth promised it would be. I savored each bite, tender and spicy. I thought of Claire at the very first taste; it was exactly the sort of dish she loves. I selected the bottle I knew Claire would have paired with it from the wine list, even though it wasn't my first choice.

"So," I said as we clinked our glasses together, "may I begin with the simplest of questions?"

"Of course."

"Why did you name your dog after him?"

Elizabeth smiled. She wasn't especially pretty, but there was something attractive about her nonetheless. It came from inside: she radiated energy and intellect. "In the big picture, your father was good to me," she said. "But when he left I was angry. I said things I later wished I had not. Percy, in retrospect, was not a man you spent your life with. He was more like a comet that flashed and left a bit of illumination behind. My life was better for having known him, but I didn't figure that out until after he died. I regretted never making peace with him, so I named Percy in his honor, meant with respect and love." She paused and put her hand to her mouth. "My goodness, what you must think. I named a *dog* after your father."

I smiled. "Freud would say you wanted to finally be able to tell him what to do."

"Freud would probably be right," she said, raising her glass to her lips, "but that isn't the only reason. I truly do remember him fondly.

He was what he was. If I expected him to be otherwise, that was more my mistake than his."

The waiter was clearing the dishes from our first course, and as he refilled our wineglasses I noticed she had finished a good deal more of hers than I had of mine. She took another long sip as soon as her glass was filled, closing her eyes as she drank with a satisfied sigh.

"Did my father drink a lot?" I asked.

"How are you defining 'a lot'?"

"As much as you?"

She batted her eyes. "Are you suggesting I drink a lot?"

"Do you?"

"Why yes, I do," she said, and raised her glass toward me for emphasis. "Your father did not. He drank a great deal of coffee. Not too much wine."

"That's what I thought."

Elizabeth ordered roasted chicken with Brussels sprouts; I had grilled salmon with broccoli. We finished a bottle of Claire's favorite Pinot Grigio and ordered another. I watched her as she drank: she seemed to savor each taste as though it was her first, and while she must have polished off an entire bottle you would not have known it from her behavior.

"How did you meet my father?" I asked.

"I knocked on his door and called him an asshole."

"Seriously?"

"Not exactly," she said. "But that's the way I like to tell the story. I assume you know I was a doctor. A damn good one, in fact. In retrospect I would have done more good for the world if I had remained one, but then I would never have met your father."

"And your dog would have a different name."

"Precisely." She took another sip of wine. "I was working in the emergency room of a hospital in the worst section of Washington. Two o'clock in the morning on a Thursday, a woman in the final stage of labor was wheeled into the ER. She was a mess. Poorly nourished, filthy, bruising on various parts of her body including the face, crack cocaine in her system. Little surprise, her child was born with all sorts of problems, a predictable result of the mother's health and lack of prenatal care. We did everything we could for that child. To my dismay, the mother was allowed to take her home when she was discharged. A month later, we received word that the mother had found a lawyer to file suit against the hospital, and every one of us on duty, when the baby was delivered. I was saddened but not concerned. Surely, anyone would be able to see what had happened. That's why I was so appalled when I was told our insurance company was going to settle the case rather than fight it. I demanded an explanation and was told a lawyer would have the mother cleaned up, there would be testimony as to the condition of the baby, and ultimately the jury would feel sympathy and give her a whole bunch of money, regardless of the real liability. I said I refused to be a part of that; I wanted to fight. They said I was welcome to fight but I would be on my own. They were going to settle and that was that. The mother ultimately got a million dollars and all of us on duty received informal reprimands. That galled me more than the money. I walked out the door and never went back."

All the time Elizabeth spoke she never raised her voice.

"So you knocked on my father's door?" I asked.

"Sort of," she said. "Percy was not only the most powerful man in Washington, he was also the most accessible. He set aside a day every month to meet with ordinary citizens to hear their ideas and their problems. Six months after that baby was born, he met with me. I was volunteering as a lobbyist for tort reform. I was scheduled for fifteen minutes of his time. I wound up spending two hours in his office and he hired me a few weeks later, told me I was the brightest person he had ever encountered. Two years later, I managed his campaign for reelection."

"When did you become romantically involved with him?"

Her face changed then, the way women's faces do when they think of a man they once loved. "Jonathan," she said, her voice more girlish,

"I assume you know that every woman that ever encountered Percy fell in love with him immediately."

"I've figured that out," I said. "I want to know why. I want to know who he was so I can understand why he did the things he did."

Elizabeth was still in girlish mode. "Your father was charming, brilliant, and powerful, which are wonderful qualities. But the real key to his appeal was none of those. Do you want to know what it was?"

I leaned closer. "Of course I do."

"He was more vulnerable than any man I've ever encountered," she said. "Women are accustomed to men who want us, but there is nothing quite as irresistible as a man who *needs* us."

Claire's face jumped into my mind. Did she *need* me? Or did I need her? "I'm not getting that part," I said. "In what way did he need you?"

"Your father could never be alone. You know that term 'serial monogamist'? That was Percy. He went from woman to woman, faithful to us until he was done with us, and then was on to the next."

"He wasn't faithful to my mother," I said.

"I know. He told me that was a great regret. He considered himself a man of principle, and he was terribly sorry he hurt your mother that way. I never met her but he spoke glowingly of her. She must have been a special person."

"Still is."

She smiled. "How nice."

The waiter approached with eyebrows raised and dessert menus in his hands. Elizabeth ordered a decaffeinated espresso; I asked for an order of tiramisu and two forks.

"Listen," Elizabeth said, "I'm going to tell you the truth about your father because you deserve to know it. When we met I fell for him immediately and he for me; I could sense it during our very first conversation. He was married to his former secretary at the time, and he was bored to tears with their relationship. He married her because she idolized him, and because she had a great ass. Christine is a lovely person but she's very limited intellectually."

"I met her," I said.

Elizabeth nodded. "Then you know. When I met your father he was starving for more than she could give him. He desperately wanted to discuss books, art, business, anything. He was a diverse, interesting man who required stimulation in more than the one way she was able to provide it."

"So he was bored?"

"He was beyond bored. He was desperate."

"Why did he marry her in the first place?"

"Because she was the opposite of your mother. Alice, from all I've heard, challenged him. She was attracted to him largely because they shared the same political views, and half the time she understood the issues better than he did. She wasn't especially impressed by his power. Christine was enormously impressed. She thought the sun rose and set around him. I've never met your mother, but I'm guessing she's not like that."

I smiled. "You couldn't be less like that than my mother."

"That's what I figured," Elizabeth said. "He married Christine because she wasn't your mother. And he married me because I wasn't Christine."

The desserts arrived, and Elizabeth stirred a cube of sugar into her coffee. I had one question remaining. "What did you mean when you said he was vulnerable?"

Elizabeth breathed a heavy sigh, remembering something that filled her with regret. "Your father could not be alone. He wouldn't do anything alone. It's the reason he didn't leave Christine before he met me, or leave me until he had found his next partner. He couldn't stand to be alone, even for an evening. He would joke about it. He'd say, 'I find my own company tedious,' and everyone would laugh. But it wasn't funny. Your father was scared to death of being alone. There's nothing at all funny about that."

I WALKED HER TO her car after we finished, and when she offered her hand for a shake I pulled her close and kissed her firmly on the cheek. When all was said and done there was a hollow quality about her; for all her vibrancy and intelligence it was clear she was a lonely person. And her emptiness was contagious. The weight of my lies and the distance I had traveled collapsed upon me like a heavy coat as I watched her drive away. Suddenly, I missed Claire terribly. I could picture her sleeping soundly in our room, buried beneath a comforter. Claire has the amazing capacity to be cold no matter the temperature and sleeps in a sweatshirt every night, bundled beneath a blanket so thick I perspire at the sight of it. But she sleeps sweetly, with a smile on her lips, and perfectly still, in keeping with her personality. She sleeps soundly, too, never budging at the shrill of my alarm or a honking car horn or fireworks on New Year's Eve. The only sounds that rouse her are ones made by the children; remarkably, a sniffle from a bedroom separated from ours by a long hallway never escapes her attention.

I desperately needed to get home, but that wasn't an option until morning. I was also exhausted, but I couldn't bear the idea of going back to the hotel and sitting alone in the darkness, waiting in vain to be overtaken by sleep. The night was warm so I thought I would just walk, as I had the night before, without a destination.

On Hopkins Avenue I passed a sign that screamed ASPEN BREWING CO. I dropped onto a stool and ordered a microbrew, choosing the brand by the look of the label. The beer was cold and buttery without a hint of bitterness; I drank half the bottle in two long sips and motioned to the bartender that I wanted another.

"This one's on the hottie over there," he said, pointing to the corner of the bar as he slid the beer my way.

"What?" I said, confused.

He fixed me with a look that suggested I was either drunk or stupid. "The attractive young woman seated over there would like to buy you a drink."

I turned; she smiled. The light gleamed off the steel rod in her tongue. "Fancy meeting you here," I said as I slid onto the stool beside hers.

"I'm always here. You're the surprise."

"Maybe it was meant to be." The bartender slid my fresh beer across the bar. "You look great."

"Thank you."

"You aren't paying for this," I said. "I'm too old to allow you to buy me a drink. In my generation the gentleman buys the lady the drink."

"That's sexism."

"No, it's good manners."

"Sometimes I get those confused."

I sipped the beer. "Your name is Amanda, right?" I said.

She smiled. "I knew I made an impression on you."

"I have a question."

"I probably have an answer."

"What made you decide to pierce your tongue?"

"It was a Wednesday and I was bored."

"No, I'm being serious."

"So am I."

I drank half the beer in a large gulp. "Do you ever regret it?"

She shook her head.

"Does it serve a purpose?"

Her smile turned sexy. "Be nice to me and you might find out." As she had in the morning, she made me stir.

"Any ink?" I asked.

"Plenty." She turned her right wrist over so her palm faced the ceiling. Just below the heel of her hand was what appeared to be a Chinese symbol.

"What is it?"

"It means *breathe*," she said. "When I get stressed, it reminds me."

"That it?"

Amanda stood. "Not even close." She slipped past me, near enough that her breasts pressed into my shoulder. I could see another tattoo at the small of her back as she walked toward the ladies' room. The bartender brought two more beers. I thought of Shelby, lying naked in the bathtub. She had been beautiful but empty. Amanda wasn't empty. She wasn't as pretty as Shelby, but she was sexier.

When Amanda came back from the bathroom she brushed against me again as she slid back onto her stool. "Miss me?" she asked.

"Terribly." We clinked our bottles together. "I saw the tattoo on your lower back," I said, "but I couldn't figure it out."

"Maybe you weren't staring hard enough." She turned away, pushed her bottom toward me. "See," she said, "it's a butterfly."

It was, an oblong butterfly. Perched atop the lacy black strap of her thong. "You know," I said, "I really regret not growing up in this era. When I was your age, girls wore leg warmers *over* their jeans. Huge, baggy Benetton sweaters with upturned collars underneath and knitted woolen stockings over their pants."

"I've seen pictures," Amanda said. "Fashion was so weird back in the day."

"There are nuns today who show more skin than a promiscuous high school girl did in 1985," I said. "Fathers must have had it so much easier back then."

"Are you a father?" she asked.

I didn't answer that. Instead I just looked down at the bar. Someone had engraved initials in it with a knife. A small puddle of dried ketchup was next to the initials. I could see my daughter's eyes in the ketchup. I was missing home again, piercingly.

"How old are you?" Amanda asked.

I could feel the beer grow warmer in my glass. "How old do you think I am?"

"I don't really care," she said. "Thirty?"

I reached for my beer, took a small sip. "A little older than that."

"Are you married?"

I lifted my left hand. The bar light reflected off my wedding ring.

"Do you care about that?"

"Of course I do."

The beer had gone totally flat, the taste bitter. All the air was out of the room, at least in the space that separated us. I stood, took two twenty-dollar bills from my pocket and dropped them on the bar. "I've really enjoyed talking with you," I said.

"Where you going?" she asked, though she didn't seem upset to see me leaving.

"I just really need to get home."

SUNDAY

"SUNDAY MEANS FAMILY!"

Drew shouted it the moment I entered the house; he can hear the garage doors from the couch where he watches television. Kids pick up on everything, even things you don't. I never consciously decided I was going to announce, "Sunday means family!" It just worked out that way, and obviously he noticed and now was repeating what he'd heard.

Claire was over for a kiss before I set down my briefcase and keys. "How are you feeling?" she asked, and pressed the back of her hand against my forehead.

"I'm not sick."

"I'll be the judge of that."

"Are you a doctor?"

"I'm a mother," she said. "That's even better." She turned back toward the kitchen but I grabbed her arm and pulled her close, kissed her hard on the lips.

"Didn't see that!" Phoebe called, turning the corner from the kitchen and shielding her eyes from the worst of all possible sights: her mother and father kissing.

"How are you, sweetheart?" I asked her.

"I'm going to kick your butt today."

"I see," I said, loosening my tie. "It's going to be like that."

Sunday nights are family nights in our house, and what that has come to mean is heavily competitive board games. Our usual routine: Claire prepares dinner, we sit to eat, she and I share a bottle of wine, the kids alternate who gets to choose the game. We play for hours and it can get heated. Claire and I made an agreement early on that we would not let the kids win, so we play hard and feelings are never spared. Sundays have often been known to end with one or both children in tears over losing, but within a few minutes that usually passes and the few moments of discontent are easily outweighed by the hours of fun.

"We're playing Scrabble tonight," Phoebe said.

"And we're having chicken, it'll be ready in twenty minutes," Claire said. "Can you open a bottle of something sensational?"

I nodded to them both. I never realized just how much they look alike. Their features mostly aren't similar, but there is something in the way it all comes together that is indescribably the same. When my daughter was born I hoped she would grow up just like her mother, and she has. She is exactly what I wanted her to be. So is Drew. So is the wine, and the chicken, and the Scrabble. And so is Claire. I couldn't escape that. As I selected a bottle of Louis Jadot Batard-Montrachet from the cellar and removed the cork, I thought: *Maybe my life is still perfect.* Then I tasted a sip of wine and took what may have been my first truly deep breath in five days.

Back in the kitchen, I handed a glass to Claire. She received it gratefully and took a sip. Our eyes met over our glasses, and in hers I saw everything I had been aching for in Aspen: familiarity, understanding, compassion. Then she winked at me, took another sip, set her glass on the counter, and went back to preparing dinner. I turned to the family room, where I saw only the backs of my kids' heads as they lay sprawled on the sofa watching television. I walked closer, holding my glass, and laid my free hand on each of them, one at a time, stroking their hair. Then I picked up the remote control and clicked the television off. "Come on, you two," I said, "let's sit at the table and talk. I feel like I've been gone forever."

There was a little grumbling, which always comes with being made to shut off the television, but they were happy to see me. Maybe not as happy as I was, but happy nonetheless. I poured two glasses of milk and the three of us took seats around the kitchen table, surrounded by the aroma of garlic and the sound of Claire rattling through silverware. In a moment she would ask the kids to set the table. The last vestiges of sunlight streamed through the windows, warming our faces. "Let's talk," I said as the kids drank their milk. "I'm interested in anything either of you has to say."

MONDAY

IT IS MY AIRBORNE observation that people in coach are happier than people in first class. I don't have an explanation, but it is too consistent to be coincidental.

I fly a great deal. With Bruce I use the private jet, but the rest of the time I am on the airlines, and what is inescapable is that the passengers in first class are cross, curt, frazzled, short with the flight attendants, and frequently downright rude, as though the pressure of maintaining their status has become too much to bear. Alternatively, the masses who are granted permission to board only after we have settled disagreeably into our seats are almost always greatly spirited, engaged in pleasant conversation, and occasionally even laughing.

"What row are we in, Daddy?" a little girl will ask, wheeling a knapsack, a stuffed animal in the crook of her elbow.

"Thirty-four," her father replies. "All the way in the back."

Nine out of ten times, that father's disposition is markedly more pleasant than that of the businessman seated beside me, nose buried in his e-mail, entire presence emitting the unmistakable vibe that if you want to have a friendly conversation you have come to the wrong place. He seems a good deal more concerned with wedging his elbow increasingly toward me in a silent but hostile bid to claim our mutual armrest simply because he is competitive that way and assumes if he doesn't I will.

As the sun rose Monday morning, I found that guy beside me as I flew out of New York. I had tiptoed out of my bedroom before five o'clock, successfully allowing Claire to sleep through my departure, in part out of consideration and the other part because I wasn't fully convinced of my skills as a liar. It is one thing to type untrue texts. It is another entirely to stare her in the face and tell her I was headed to the office when in reality I was rushing to catch a flight to Saint Kitts, West Indies.

I landed on the island just before eleven o'clock and was transported via ferry three miles across a shallow channel to the island of Nevis. I had heard of the Four Seasons Resort Nevis, but until one is making the approach on a sun-drenched morning it is not possible to fully appreciate the spectacle of the signature red umbrellas set against the sugary white beach and translucent turquoise sea. *The children would love it here,* I thought as the wind rushed through my hair and a light mist coated my face. But I would never bring them. Not after today. There are other places with white beaches and blue water; I wouldn't need to revisit all this baggage just to get a suntan.

At the dock I was greeted with a smile and a tropical drink, then escorted to my room, which overlooked the tennis courts. The first tee was just beyond, lush and green, with white-bellied monkeys dancing in the trees. There was a scuba lesson going on at one end of the swimming pool, an exercise class at the other; water-skiers were loading a speedboat off the shore, and a steel drum band played a reggae version of "Leaving on a Jet Plane" adjacent to the luncheon buffet.

"As you can see, the variety of activities has no limit," said the pleasant young man who showed me to my room. "Is there anything I can add to your schedule?"

"Thanks, no," I replied. "I only came here to do yoga."

THE ENTRANCE TO THE spa was just off the tennis courts and looked exactly like the waiting area of every spa I have ever seen: glass walls, running water, chimes, new-age music, a table bearing signature lotions, creams, oils, gels, shampoo, bath beads.

A tall, dark-haired woman behind the appointment desk raised a hand as I entered. "Good afternoon," she said. "May I help you with anything?"

"I'm here for the noon yoga."

"Yoga with Miss Anne is in the garden by the reflecting pool. She'll be here any moment. Will you require a locker?"

"Thanks, no," I said. "I'll wait outside."

"Do you have a mat?"

"I don't."

"Help yourself to one from the bin."

I pulled out a tightly rolled yoga mat and made my way into the sun. It was a cloudless day with enough breeze to take the edge off the heat, perfect for exercise. I unrolled the mat and laid it beside the small pool, pulled off my sneakers, and stood barefoot, breathing deeply in the sea air, my face upturned to the sun.

The voice came from behind me, soft but deep. "Hold that for five, four, three, two, one. Now engage the muscles of your throat as you slowly let it out through your nose. This is called our *ujjayi* breath. Find yours. Five, four, three, two, one. Very good."

I turned toward the voice, my eyes squinting in the reflection of the sun. "Are you Miss Anne?"

"I am," she said, and placed her palms together in front of her chest. "Namaste."

I bowed my head. "Namaste."

Anne was taller than I expected, with long legs and flowing gray hair. Her arms and shoulders were gracefully muscled, long and sinewy, the sort of muscle that comes from yoga rather than lifting weights. She wore black Lululemon yoga pants and an opaque T-shirt covered in symbols and three words: LOVE, LIFE, YOGA. "Appears you're the only one today," she said. "Anything in particular you'd like to do?"

All I knew of yoga came from watching my mother. "Not really," I said. "Just need a good stretch."

"Do you have any injuries I should know of? Bad back?"

I shook my head.

"Very well," she said, and extended a tiny hand. "I'm Anne Sweetwater."

"Jonathan."

"Nice to meet you, Jonathan. Let's begin in Child's Pose."

For forty minutes, Anne's soothing voice guided me through a series of yoga poses—*Adho Mukha Svanasana, Tadasana, Utkatasana, Bakasana, Setu Bandha*—softly adjusting me with her experienced hands, ever mindful of my breathing. Her manner was so serene that I didn't feel at all awkward, despite the intimacy of the interaction. For most of the hour I wasn't even thinking of her connection to my father, I was just mindful of my posture and breathing. "Deeply in, deeply out," she said time and again. For our final pose she positioned me flat on my back and ran her fingers over my face. "Eyes closed," she whispered. "Take rest."

I focused hard as I could on my breathing.

"Feel your head press deeply into your mat," she whispered. "Now your back . . . your arms . . . your legs." She ran a hand over my face again. "Give yourself to the earth."

My body was drenched in sweat but I wasn't tired. I felt relaxed and quiet, more like after a massage than a workout. The sun on my face was strong but friendly, a simple, warming glow.

"How do you feel?"

I sat up and found Anne seated in Lotus Pose by the reflecting pool, her hands again pressed together before her, head bowed, eyes closed.

"I feel wonderful," I said.

"May the sun that warms your face spread across your soul so you may warm the hearts of all those who love you." She opened her eyes and locked them deeply with mine. *"Namaste,"* she said.

"Namaste."

Her lips curled into a gentle smile. She was a strikingly beautiful woman, for any age. "I hope you enjoyed that," she said.

I scrambled to my knees. "I did, very much. I'd love to talk to you more about it."

"You are welcome to join me for lunch."

I couldn't believe my luck. "That would be fabulous."

Anne's smile grew even wider. "It will be a pleasure," she said. "And it will give us a chance to talk about your father."

UP THE BEACH A few hundred yards was Sunshine, a shack with reggae music blaring, hamburgers on a grill, and a white-bellied monkey called Frisky tied to a rope.

"How great, the monkeys," I said as we took a table in the shade.

"The kids love them."

"Why is this one tied to a rope?"

Anne smiled. "Because he would run away otherwise."

A waiter approached wearing a red apron over a white T-shirt. "Mornin', dahlin'," he said to Anne.

"It's not morning anymore."

"It is for me," the waiter said, and broke into a startling laugh.

"Say hello to Jonathan," Anne said. "I knew his father once upon a time."

"Pleased to meet you," the waiter said, extending a huge hand. "Name is Rowley." His fingers were stained yellow and smelled of smoke.

"What's the best thing on the menu, Rowley?" I asked.

"Lobster," he said. "And Killer Bees."

"Two of each," Anne said.

"What's a Killer Bee?" I asked.

Rowley laughed again, shook his head without answering, and went back behind the bar.

"What's a Killer Bee?" I asked Anne.

"You don't have any plans for later today, do you?" she asked.

I shook my head.

"Then relax, you'll love it."

I looked around. Children were playing in the sand as the waves crashed onto the beach. The breeze was steady and cool. "I can see why you love it here," I said.

"Been twenty years," she said, her hair blowing gently in the wind. "Never plan on leaving." She closed her eyes, resting her head on the back of her neck, rolling slowly one way and the other, stretching the muscles of her upper back and shoulders. "I assume you have many questions," she said.

"I do."

"What's the first one?"

"How did you know it was me?"

Her lips parted, then spread into a smile. "Your aura."

I was stunned. "What do you mean?"

"It doesn't happen often," Anne said, "but there was something strong in your presence. I could feel Percy in the air, in the breeze, in the sound of the sea. It was you that brought him, Jonathan. He was coming from you."

We were quiet for a moment before being interrupted by Rowley, who slammed two large, red drinks onto the table. Anne lifted her head, nodded politely, picked up her glass. "Welcome to Nevis, Jonathan," she said.

"This has got to be the most incredible moment of my life."

We clinked glasses and she raised hers to her lips, but before taking a sip she let out a laugh, louder than any sound I would have thought her capable of making. Her expression dripped with maternal empathy. "Jonathan, sweetheart," she said, "your yoga session was charged to your room."

"What?"

"Your room is registered to Mr. Jonathan Sweetwater. That's how I knew who you were."

I slammed the drink down on the table, harder than I intended. "You're kidding."

"I'm afraid not," she said. "I'm sorry to disappoint you. I didn't think you'd believe me in the first place, but when it seemed so important to you I couldn't let it go on."

I felt like I had been punched in the stomach. "I completely believed you," I said. "Am I going crazy?"

Anne leaned back again in her chair. "I don't know. Are you?"

THE KILLER BEE IS made with two tablespoons of honey, orange juice, club soda, passion fruit juice, black pepper, lime, and a healthy portion of light rum. The first sip is an explosion. After that the ice in the cup melts quickly and softens the flavor, so the only ingredient you do not taste is the rum no matter how many you drink; I'd had three by the time the food arrived.

The lobster was fresh and delicious, spicy in a way that blended perfectly with the passion fruit in the Killer Bee.

"You must have been pretty young when you divorced Percy," I said.

Anne's mouth was full. She covered it with her hand as she chewed. "Before we start getting into how old I am, let me make one thing abundantly clear: I most certainly did not divorce Percy. He divorced me."

"He seems to have divorced everyone."

"He was that sort of man."

"What sort of man divorces five women?" I asked.

"The sort who makes you feel like the most beautiful, desirable person in the world. And then, with no warning, moves on."

"Do you hate him?"

Anne looked away. Just a scintilla of the serenity in her face disappeared, replaced by a slight furrowing of her brow.

"It's all right with me if you do," I went on. "I don't know how much you know about me, but I had no relationship with him at all. The last time I saw Percy I was nine years old."

"I assume you came here looking for me," Anne said, still looking away. "Why?"

"So I could ask you this question exactly: Do you hate my father?"

Anne took a short sip of her drink, then leaned back again, eyes closed. She was breathing deeply, the *ujjayi* breath. "Have you heard of Thich Nhat Hanh?" she asked.

"No."

"He's a Buddhist monk, a brilliant one. He won the Nobel Prize for peace. He says that when another person makes you suffer, it is because he suffers deeply within himself and his suffering is spilling over. He says such a man does not need punishment. He needs help." Anne opened her eyes and leaned closer. "Do you want to know what I say?"

I leaned as well, so close our noses nearly touched.

"I say: Fuck Him."

She didn't smile when she said it, didn't change expression at all. Her breathing remained steady. Deeply in, deeply out. I could feel her warmth on my face.

"Do you mean Thich Nhat Hanh?" I asked.

Anne shook her head. "Of course not. Thich Nhat Hanh is a beautiful man and a genius. Your father, meanwhile, was an asshole. So fuck him."

We stayed that way, our faces close. To an observer it might have appeared we were trying to decide whether to kiss. I felt the rum tickling my brain.

"So, that's how I feel," Anne finally said, and leaned back in her chair and went back to her lobster.

"How did you meet him?" I asked. "Did Percy study yoga?"

"My goodness," she said, no longer bothering to conceal her chewing. "You really don't know anything about him, do you?"

I shook my head.

"I wasn't a yogi when I met your father," Anne said. "I was a dancer. A prima ballerina at the Washington Ballet. Have you heard of it?"

I shook my head. I hadn't. Though I did vaguely remember, now that she mentioned it, that she'd been a dancer.

"Just like your father," she sniffed, "a New York snob. The Washington Ballet is one of the foremost dance companies in the world. I danced with Twyla Tharp."

"Sorry."

Anne softened. "I was mostly teasing. Anyway, it was very simple, how we met. I was dancing. Your father came to a performance. They brought him backstage afterward to meet the company."

"Love at first sight?"

She let out a sigh. "He was something else, your father. He was sixty-five years old, but he had incredible energy and passion."

"He was married at the time?"

"He was, but I didn't know that at first. We chatted for several minutes backstage. The following night, he sent two dozen yellow roses to my dressing room. The card said: *Delightful to know you.* That was it."

"Pretty smooth."

Anne laughed lightly. "When a man sends you two dozen roses, it is a statement. When the most powerful member of the United States Senate sends them, it is a life-changing event."

"You fell in love with him?"

"My goodness, yes. The first time we dined together. He was funny and interesting. But you know the best thing about him?" She paused. "He listened. This was a man who routinely dined with presidents, heads of state. He traveled all over the globe helping to shape the world, but he listened to me. He was interested in my life. That was his gift."

"That he cared about people?"

Anne shook her head. "That he made you *think* he did."

Her life story, as she relayed it to me all these years after relaying it to my father, was not uncommon and mostly sad. She was raised by a single mother who pushed her hard to dance. She showed me her feet: gnarled, misshapen, two of the nails gray and withered. "Do you have a daughter?" she asked me.

"I do."

"Does she love to dance?"

"She does."

"Don't *force* her," Anne said. A tiny vein pulsated above her right eye. "I loved to dance when I was a girl. By the time I was in high school I hated it more than anything. The competition was unspeakable. And my mother wanted it more than I did. I was bulimic, depressed. Every cliché you've ever heard of."

"And my father made it better?"

She smiled again. "He cared about me. He loved to watch me dance but made it clear it was unimportant to him. He told me if I wanted to give it up he supported me."

"He told you that the first night?"

"Not exactly," she said. "But not long after."

"Wasn't he still married to Elizabeth?"

Her smile faded. "That is my great regret. He told me they were separated, that a divorce was a formality. I was twenty-nine years old. He was a senator. I believed him."

"But it wasn't true?"

Anne brushed away a strand of hair that had fallen over her cheek. "I'm sure it wasn't. If it was anything like the way he left me, it was the biggest surprise of her life. I never had the nerve to face her, even after all these years. I don't even know where she is."

I thought of telling her but then decided against it. Some wounds are best left untended. "So you married him," I said.

"I most certainly did. And I never set foot on a stage again. That was twenty-three years ago."

Rowley came to clear our plates. The breeze in the air had picked up. A newspaper resting on a nearby table came apart and blew away. A little boy was running in circles on the beach, wearing only a diaper, carrying a bucket filled with water. I watched him as he ran; it didn't seem possible a boy so small could remain upright as long as he did. Finally he stopped, poured the water out of his bucket, and flopped down on his butt.

"We had wonderful times together, your father and I," Anne was saying. "The press loved me, they loved our age difference. We were the Bogey and Bacall of Washington. And he didn't care at all that I wasn't dancing anymore."

"How did your mother feel about it?"

"She didn't care for it. And she didn't much care for him either. Percy was several years older than my mother. That's awkward no matter how hard you try."

"Is she still alive?"

"She is," Anne said. "She lives in Maryland. I don't see her much."

Rowley brought over a check and dropped it on the table between us. Anne began to reach for it but I snatched it away. "Please let me," I said. "And, if you don't mind, I have so much more I want to ask you."

"Let's take a walk," she said. "I don't have anywhere to be."

I dropped a hundred dollars onto the table and covered the bill with a glass.

"I have this feeling," Anne said as we walked, "that it wasn't any great coincidence you found me. You didn't just stumble into my yoga class today."

"I did not," I agreed.

"You were looking for me?"

"I was."

"After all these years. Why?"

I shrugged. "Sometimes it's enough just to know that you have to. You don't always know why."

"You want to know more about your father?"

"I want to know *something* about him."

A wave crashed gently over our ankles, past our feet, lost steam, retreated back to the ocean.

"I'll tell you something about him," Anne said. "Your father was the most restless person I've ever been around. He could not sit still. He was the sort whose foot was always tapping. On vacations he never sat on a beach and read a magazine; he was always learning, studying. He needed to accomplish something every day. In the evening he might bask in the glow of it all with a good meal, but in the morning he was right back at it again."

I thought of Claire's hands, ever still, resting on a table. "Why was he like that?" I asked.

Anne sighed. "I can tell you a lot about Percy," she said, "but that doesn't mean I can explain him. He was one of a kind."

We walked a bit in quiet. I was very comfortable in her presence. There was something soothing about Anne, quite different from either of my father's two previous wives. She reminded me more of my mother.

"How about if I ask *you* a question?" Anne said. "Is it just me you've come to see? Or did you find the others as well?"

"I'm trying to meet all of my father's wives."

Anne nodded. "I never met your mother," she said. "Or Christine, or Elizabeth. I didn't know any of Percy's other wives. If you don't mind my asking, what have you found so far?"

"I don't know," I said. "I've heard a lot of things but I don't have any idea what to make of them."

"Are we all alike?" she asked.

I stopped to think about that. They were so different in all the obvious ways, but there was one similarity. "You all seem sad," I said.

Anne reached out her small hand and gently touched it to my cheek. "You're a sweet young man," she said. "And you look more like your father than I first realized."

We were nearing the resort. Children were throwing a Frisbee, white-nosed tourists sat on lounge chairs, scuba instructors in wetsuits were taking a group into the sea. Beyond them all a solitary figure at the top of the hill looked out of place, a white-haired man in a linen shirt and jeans. As we approached he began to wave. I thought he was waving to me, but then I saw Anne's face light up. "Come," she said, and took my hand, "I'd like you to meet Val."

"Who is Val?"

"Val is the man I've been married to for the last fifteen years."

I waited for the laughter. This *had* to be another joke. "What are you talking about?" I finally asked.

"Jonathan, I'm a married woman. I assumed you knew that."

"I did not." I never envisioned anyone moving on after Percy. None of his previous wives had. In some ways, I hadn't either. "If you're remarried, why is your last name still Sweetwater?" I asked.

For the second time, Anne looked as though she felt sorry for me. "I'm going to tell you, because he's your father and you should know, but you must promise to keep the secret. Part of the agreement is that it remain a secret. Just wait here a moment."

Anne walked up the beach, quick and determined, straight toward the man in the linen shirt. I looked up at the sky. Clouds were on the horizon, forming menacingly over the volcano in the distance. The sea washed over me, almost to my knees. Up by the resort, Anne was talking with her husband, too far away to hear. After a moment she kissed him on the lips and started back toward me, more slowly now. The waves crashed over me again as she arrived.

"Let's walk some more," she said. "We still have a little while before the rain comes in from the mountain."

Anne held my hand gently as we walked. Around us resort staff was busy clearing the beach of cups and towels, while the captains of small boats covered their vessels in case the weather turned uglier than expected.

"Jonathan, your father was an unusual person. I don't know what you've heard of him from his other wives, but it was during the time I was with him that his health began to deteriorate. His heart, mostly. And, as I learned, when your heart is not functioning properly, nothing else does either. Your father became frantic as he grew older, obsessed with his legacy. That was why he couldn't rest. I didn't want to mention it earlier, but I see now that you came all this way because you want answers, not a sugarcoated vision of a legend."

The breeze picked up, blew the collar of my shirt onto my neck. "That's right," I said.

"When he left he gave me more money than I could ever imagine. We never went to court; he didn't even use a lawyer. Businesspeople handled the entire transaction. He had only one demand. I assumed it would be that I never speak ill of him publicly, but he wasn't at all concerned about that. His only stipulation was that I maintained his name for the rest of my life."

I felt a raindrop on my cheek, brushed it away. "I don't understand," I said.

"I don't know that I do either. He didn't explain it, and I didn't ask him to. He offered me five million dollars and all I had to do was sign an agreement that I would never legally change my name. I signed it, he kissed me on the forehead, and I never saw him again."

It was raining now, a light but consistent sprinkle. I was thinking of a discussion Claire and I had the morning after we became engaged. She asked if it would upset me if she did not legally take my name. I pretended it would not even though it did. I asked her why it was important to her. She told me it was because her parents had no other children. I asked why that was so important. She said: "I don't know, it just is." She never did legally take the name Sweetwater.

Anne and I turned back toward the resort, but we weren't walking any faster. The rain wasn't a good enough reason to hurry. "Val doesn't mind?" I asked.

Anne smiled sweetly at the mention of his name. "Blissfully, he does not."

"Does he treat you well?" I asked. "Does he make you happier than my father did?"

Anne stopped, wrapped her fingers even more tightly around mine. "Val treats me wonderfully and I love him with all my heart. But, Jonathan, no one will ever make me happier than your father did, and that's just the truth."

I opened my mouth but no sound came out.

"How about you, Jonathan? Are you married?" she asked.

"I am."

"Does your wife make you happier than anyone else possibly could?"

The weight of the question made my voice small. "She really does."

"Then make sure she knows it," Anne said. "Never let her go."

There wasn't anything further to be said and we both knew it, so neither of us tried. In a moment we would make our way back to the resort and say good-bye. But for now, we were fine where we were. Total strangers, bound only by a man neither of us really knew, standing on a beach, holding hands in the rain.

TUESDAY

I LANDED AT KENNEDY airport just before noon and took a taxi to my mother's apartment. I stopped at the same café on the corner and picked up two ham-and-cheese croissants, two sides of vinaigrette potato salad, and two cups of black coffee. I rang the buzzer with my elbow.

Her voice crackled through the intercom. "Jonathan?"

"You guessed it."

"Please tell me you didn't bring food."

"I brought food."

There was a pause. "Oh, for heaven's sake," she said, and buzzed me in.

A moment later the locks were crackling and sliding and then the door opened before me. Instantly, my heart rose. Mother was dressed, her hair done, her makeup in place; she looked ten years younger than the last time I'd seen her.

"Why are you staring at me?" she asked. "Is something wrong with my appearance?"

"No," I said. "Everything is about where it's supposed to be."

"What the hell does that mean?"

I shook my head. "Just something Claire says all the time."

Mother grabbed the paper bag from my hand. "How are we making me fat today?" she asked.

"Low-calorie sandwiches," I said. "Mom, you look terrific."

"That's because this is a human time of day to ring a woman's doorbell," she said. "Go knock on Gisele's door at seven in the morning and tell me how gorgeous *she* looks."

I sat at the kitchen table, the sunlight streaming through the skylights, and Mother brought two plates, two forks, skim milk for the coffee, and a stack of napkins. "So," she said as she sat across from me. "Now what?"

I poured milk into my coffee, watched the color change. "I've had quite a week."

"It's only Tuesday."

I took a sip. "Still," I said, "you wouldn't believe the places I've been."

Mother took a small, careful bite of her sandwich. She is perfectly comfortable in silence. Claire is the same way. They can both pause in the middle of a conversation and wait, interminably if need be.

"I've met three of Percy's wives," I said.

If Mother was surprised her face did not show it. She just kept chewing slowly. "Does that or does it not include me?"

My heart skipped. It hadn't occurred to me that Mother might think of my journey as a betrayal. "I hope this doesn't upset you," I said.

She cackled. "Oh, Jonathan, sometimes the only way to handle a moment of discomfort is with humor. I learned that a long time ago from a pretty smart fellow you may have heard of."

"Do you want to know about them?" I asked.

Mother took another sip of coffee. "Not really," she said. "But if you learned anything from the experience, I would very much like to hear about that."

"I learned a great deal," I said. "I just have no idea what it means."

Mother waited again. Took a bite, chewed, never averted her eyes.

"I was hoping to find some thread of commonality among all of them," I said, "but I didn't. The only thing that unites them is Percy."

"What more did you expect?"

"I don't know."

Mother sighed. "Sweetheart, I applaud you for making the effort, and I understand why you felt you had to do it. If my math is correct you still have two more to go, and I wouldn't discourage you from trying. But please understand that all you may do is discover more about your father."

"What else is there?"

"I feel like you're out there in search of yourself. Or of Claire," she said. "You won't find those by meeting Percy's wives."

"Then how do I find them?"

"Jonathan," she said, "the only questions that are really worth asking are the ones we cannot answer."

I looked down at my hands. For a change, they were perfectly still. "Did Percy say that?"

Mother slammed her fist on the table; the noise caught me off guard. "I assume you realize your father said a great many brilliant things." There was frustration in her voice. "That doesn't have to be such a burden. You are a smart, responsible man and I couldn't be more proud of you, but when it comes to your father it's time for you to grow up."

"I don't know how."

"How to do what?"

"I don't know how to be older," I said. "All I've ever been is younger."

Mother rose and pulled her chair closer to mine. "Here is the most important lesson you need to learn from your father," she said. "The key to life is learning to put up with the imperfections. If you expect life to be perfect, you will always be disappointed. If you expect *yourself* to be perfect, you will never be satisfied. And if you expect *others* to be perfect, you will always be alone."

"Did Percy say that?"

She squeezed my shoulder. "No, my dear, I am pleased to tell you he did not. Those were my own observations. About him, and about you."

"So, I'm just like my father?"

"In this regard, yes you are. Both of you, in your own way, are always chasing perfect. That's how you wound up where you are right now."

"And how about Percy?"

Mother smiled. "That's how he ended up with six wives."

I COULDN'T BEAR THE thought of going to the office. Even basketball didn't appeal to me; I was weary, drained. Nor could I fathom boarding another airplane. There was one more trip remaining, but that would have to wait. What I needed more than anything was a night in my own bed.

First, though, I would go to school. Sonny would drive me straight there, then he would take us all to the ice cream shop; I wasn't stopping at the house for my car.

Sonny is notable for two reasons: his speed and his odor. On this day, he outdid himself in both areas. He made it from lower Manhattan to Westport in just forty minutes, and we rode the entire distance with my window down; it was with great relief that I stepped from the car into the sunshine of the school parking lot. In ten minutes the bell would ring and release a flood of noisy, joyous children in alligator shirts and plaid skirts, lugging oversized backpacks, laughing loudly about anything and nothing, mostly pleased just to have completed another day of school.

"Find a place to sit," I shouted into the open car window. "It'll be a few minutes."

Sonny nodded amiably and pulled away, vigilant in his carefulness.

On the highway he was a man possessed, but there was a real sweetness in the way he inched through a school parking lot, as though at any moment an unwitting child might spontaneously appear.

I couldn't think of anything better than a few minutes of total silence, so I headed for my favorite, most secluded place, a wooden bench dedicated to a beloved science teacher beneath a sturdy oak in a garden between the playground and soccer fields. The garden is barely visible from the school or the parking lot, the perfect place to be alone. Which is why I was so disappointed, as well as surprised, when I came around the tree to find Claire seated on the bench.

I stopped dead in my tracks and stared at the back of her head. Every question I wanted to ask flooded my brain. I longed to share with her everything that had happened, about Shelby and Amanda, and all of Percy's wives. I wanted her to assure me that anything I thought I had seen was a mistake, there was a simple explanation, that everything was exactly as it had always been and would always be. I opened my mouth to speak, but before the words came pouring forth I realized there was something different about Claire. It was something in the way her hair fell, perhaps to the wrong side. And it was just a bit longer than it should have been. Then she lifted her arm and rested it along the top of the bench, still facing away, and the instant I saw her rings I realized why she appeared different. It was because it wasn't Claire at all. And it was the second time I had made that mistake.

The first was eighteen months ago, beneath an overcast sky. It was Art Night at school, where soft drinks and brownies are served while all the students' paintings are displayed on the walls. Sonny dropped me off just outside the entrance and I hurried in, rejoicing in the sound of the chaos, relieved I wasn't too late. In the dim light I saw my wife outside a classroom. I stepped stealthily toward her and patted her gently on the behind.

"Hello, beautiful," I said in a sexy voice.

She turned her head and only her head, and the smile on my face froze, as did my hand, still resting on her ass. I couldn't move, so I didn't, and neither did she, and then she winked and shook her hair. "Hello to you too, handsome," she said.

It wasn't Claire, of course. It was Betsy Buchanan. And what I remember most is the way she reacted. She didn't appear embarrassed or insulted or even amused; if I wasn't mistaken, she was excited. Ever since that day, Betsy's friendliness has turned flirtatious in my presence. Rather than pretend the whole thing never happened, she instead jokes about it constantly, in a manner that sometimes feels like an invitation. I perceive Betsy to be a lonely woman. Her husband is significantly older, a former surgeon with grown children from a previous marriage. He travels the world constantly, lecturing and teaching a procedure for which he is renowned. Amiable and obviously smart, he is without a hint of warmth, the opposite of his outgoing, enthusiastic bride. It has never been clear to me where the two of them meet in the middle, not that the matter is any of my concern, but I've been acutely aware of it ever since the night I fondled her butt.

That was the first time I'd mistaken her for Claire. Now, here on the bench at school, it had happened again.

"Hi, Jon," she said. Her voice was husky.

"Do you mind if I sit?" I asked. "I've had a very long week."

She slid to the side and tapped the empty space with waggling fingers. "Tell me," she said. "What has been keeping us so busy?"

"You know," I said, staring at the grass beneath our feet, "all the usual things."

"Yes, the usual things are exhausting. It's the *unusual* things that keep us awake."

A chipmunk darted up the trunk of a tree. A car horn sounded. Two women passed behind us on the path, speaking softly.

"Where is Mitchell?" I asked. Mitchell is her husband.

"Prague," she said. "I think."

A group of birds passed above in formation, casting a moving shadow across the lawn. Betsy slid slightly toward me, almost imperceptibly. Her arm was still on the back of the bench, her hand beside my ear.

"You look like you might fall asleep," she said.

"I'm fine." The bell was going to ring any second; you could feel it in the silence in the air. "Are *you* fine?" I asked.

I saw the muscles in Betsy's throat tighten. "Of course I am," she said, and looked away. "You know, I was voted the hottest mom in the tenth grade. What more does a girl need than that?"

I didn't know what to say. Claire would never have cared about such a thing as being considered sexy by a bunch of fifteen-year-old boys. I was trying to figure out how to respond when I noticed there were tears in Betsy's eyes. I guess if you aren't quite sure that your husband is in Prague, things just aren't as they should be.

Finally the bell rang and the sound hung in the air, filling the last moments of tranquillity. I put my hand on Betsy's shoulder and squeezed gently. She smiled and stood, and lingered just a moment, her butt inches from my face, long enough to remind me that she remembered. Then she walked away toward the courtyard, where the voices of the youngest students were already reaching a crescendo.

I waited long enough to take two deep breaths, then got up myself. I passed Sonny on my way through the parking lot, standing beside the car, speaking into a cell phone. Behind him a group of older boys were crowding around a van that was blasting music, the school logo painted on the side. The soccer team, I thought. I didn't recognize Betsy's eldest son among them, but I knew it to be his group. And I saw Betsy a few steps ahead of me, walking alone, slowing as she passed the boys, shaking her hips a little in time with the music.

AFTER THE ICE CREAM, the basketball, the homework, the Boggle, grilled salmon, warm chocolate chip cookies, an hour of television, and only a little struggle getting the kids up to bed, Claire and I were alone in the dining room. The table was covered with dirty dishes, and we were savoring glasses of Grgich Hills Chardonnay. Claire's eyes rolled back each time she raised the glass to her lips; she loves wine even more than I do.

"You going to be home for a little while?" she asked.

"One more trip," I said. "London. Then it should be done for a while."

She sighed. "So much travel. Don't forget the kids' concert is Thursday night."

"I'll be back for it, for sure."

She sloshed about her glass and raised it beneath her nose, then smacked her lips. "You must be exhausted."

"Do I look exhausted?"

She looked me up and down. "Actually, no," she said. "Everything is about where it should be."

Her lips were close to mine, full and moist; she was so beautiful I could hardly bear it. The sight of her face, the smell of the cookies, the feel of the glass in my hands. I leaned forward and kissed her, passionately. She kissed me back, then began to withdraw. "Jonathan," she said, "the dishes."

"Leave them."

"We *can't* leave them."

I could smell the wine on her breath. "We can. I know it seems unusual, but that doesn't mean it can't be done."

"Jonathan, don't be crazy."

I pressed my lips to hers again. "People do far crazier things every day."

"Just a second," she said, and started toward the kitchen, but I didn't let her get there. I jumped behind and lifted her off the ground.

"Jonathan," she whispered, "the kids."

"They're asleep," I said. "I promise." She went limp in my arms. I turned abruptly and headed for the stairs.

"We cannot leave the dishes sitting there all night," she said.

"Maybe we won't," I said. "Maybe we'll come down later and make hot fudge sundaes. I just can't think that far ahead."

I carried her up the stairs and turned left, into our bedroom, without so much as a glance in the other direction. I wasn't concerned with what had happened there. I was thinking only of right now. I kicked the door shut behind us and dropped her softly onto the bed. The moonlight streaming through the windows cast a black and white shadow as she wriggled out of her jeans. I was out of my clothes quickly too and collapsed on top of her; I heard the air go out of her chest, but the smile never left her face. I wanted to feel her skin against mine and I did, soft and warm and familiar. I held her as though I would never let go, and as we began to make love I once again heard my father's voice. This time he was telling me I had it right. Everything really was right where it was supposed to be.

WEDNESDAY

THE MORE TIME I spend in London, the more I find the need to remind myself I am not in New York. More than any other city, foreign or domestic, London feels like my hometown. So, despite all the traveling I had done, when I stepped into the taxi at Heathrow my mind was quiet.

I spent the ride from the airport checking e-mail and arranging a calendar that had been thrown into a state of flux by the events of the past week. One e-mail from Bruce was of particular significance. *Need you here tomorrow 1p.*

It wasn't a request, and it left me very little time. I would need to be on the first flight back to Kennedy in the morning, which meant I absolutely had to find her tonight.

I took a room at the Berkeley Hotel on Wilton Place, a mile from Piccadilly Circus, in Knightsbridge. I had stayed in numerous hotels in London through the years, but never this one. This time I had chosen not for the elegance but rather the location.

I dropped my bag in the hotel room and headed out into the evening air. It was uncharacteristically pretty for London, a city in which the sky can almost never be described as "pretty." But it was clear with just a few clouds, and the air was brisk but not cold. I hiked the collar of my jacket toward my ears. There was no need for an overcoat.

Directly across from the hotel was Kinnerton Street, a narrow, diagonal path, removed from the bustle of Knightsbridge by only a few steps and yet seemingly of an entirely other place and time. Tiny flats, potted plants, a small grocery selling milk and premade ham salad sandwiches. A group of men in suits were outside a pub drinking beer and smoking cigarettes, laughing loudly. I was overwhelmed by the smoke as I passed. The men, no longer allowed to smoke inside, took enormous puffs on their cigarettes with no regard at all for passersby. The smell was bitter and powerful, stronger than the smoke back home. Perhaps this was one small difference between London and New York: in New York the smokers have the decency to feel guilty as they ruin your walk.

Just beyond the pub was a small wooden sign: JUDITH BLACKLOCK FLOWER SCHOOL. Delightfully, once I turned into the alley, the revelry and smoke vanished instantly, replaced by a quietude much more in keeping with my state of mind. And the window of the flower shop was nothing short of spectacular. I'm not one who is always observant of such things, but the beauty of this display was impossible to miss, the shapes and colors electrifying, splashes of red, purple, and yellow, crystal vases, leafy greens, whites around the edges. I paused a moment to take it all in.

A bell rang as I pushed open the door. The smell was sensational, as sweet as the smoke had been bitter, perhaps even more so. I was reminded of when Phoebe was younger, and one of her favorite activities was strolling through the flower shop near our house, smelling the flowers and playing with the small cat that belonged to the owners. She would drag me from vase to vase, burying her face in the bouquets, taking long, exaggerated sniffs.

A cheerful voice, straight out of a British sitcom, came from behind a door. "You just made it, almost closing time. I'll be right with you." From behind the cluttered desk emerged exactly the woman you would expect to find in such a shop: small, blond hair in a bun, reading glasses perched atop her head, apron, shears, heavy accent. "So sorry," she said, frazzled but not anxious. "Two weddings this weekend, just about up to my ears. How can I be of service?"

"Are you Judith?" I asked.

"Indeed I am."

"It's a pleasure to meet you. I'm Jonathan. I just have a few questions . . ."

"We cover every single aspect of flowers," she interrupted cheerily. "We teach classes in floral design, which is for amateur use, or floristry, which is for professionals. We have a two-week course, after which you will never need another lesson to open your own shop or do events like weddings or *funerals*." Her voice dropped significantly on the last word. No one likes funerals, but Judith seemed the sort of person who especially disliked them. "Are you interested in the class?" she asked.

"Not right now," I said. "I'm looking for Ciara Cavanaugh."

Judith grinned. "I've never met a man who wasn't."

"Is she here?"

"Not right now. What business have you with her?"

"Is she the owner?"

"In a manner of speaking, she is. You looking to buy the place? Because I'll tell you now, she's not going to sell."

"I'm not looking to buy anything. It's . . . a personal matter."

The smile on Judith's face waned. "She might be in tomorrow. You can come back then. I need to close up around here, if you don't mind." She walked past me toward the door, perhaps to hasten my exit, perhaps to bolt for safety if I really was the lunatic she had decided I might be.

"Listen," I said, "I just need to talk to her. I promise you I'm not dangerous, or crazy. She was married to my father, and I never met her. That's all."

Judith cocked her head to one side, just as Claire always does when trying to size up a situation. "You talking about the senator?"

"Yes. He was my father."

Her eyes narrowed. "What was his name?"

"Percy," I said.

She nodded. "Listen, I don't know about just sending strangers over to Ciara's place. She's got stalkers, you know."

"I'm not a stalker. I just want to talk with her. Can you just call her and tell her I'm here? She might want to meet me."

Judith's skepticism was fading, but she didn't move from the door.

"Tell you what," I said. "I will wait outside if you prefer. Please call her and tell her Jonathan Sweetwater, Percy's son, is here. I just want to ask her about a few things."

"You're not going to try to claim ownership of the shop, are you?"

I smiled, gently as I could. "I promise you I am not."

She looked me up and down, sizing me up, and finally nodded. "All right," she said. "You seem okay to me. Hold on." She pulled a cell phone from a pocket in her apron, pushed her glasses down over her eyes, and typed furiously with her thumbs. Then she looked up at me. "I'll hear back in just . . ."

Her phone reverberated before she could finish. She looked down at the screen again. "She'll be here in five minutes," she said, the cheer back in her voice. "Would you like to see the shop while you wait?"

Judith poured a glass of lemonade and walked me through the entire floral spectrum. She was very knowledgeable, and generally chatty as well, particularly on the subject of Ciara Cavanaugh. "She saved my life," Judith said. "I owe everything I have to her."

When I heard the bells over the door jingle I was behind a wall of orchids, soaking in the fragrance. I came out the other side to find Ciara in the doorway. She took my breath away.

I had seen photos, of course. Everyone has seen photos. In my youth, Ciara Cavanaugh was the world's most famous fashion model.

The decades that had passed had, if anything, only added to her strik-
ing beauty, imbuing her features with a richness and complexity. Her
hair was chestnut brown and up in a bun, loose strands dangling on
either side of her eyes. Her trademark cheekbones were as prominent
as ever. And while she was smaller than I had expected, her presence
was larger than life.

"Sweet Jesus," she said. "Johnny boy, after all these years, look at
you."

"Pleasure to meet you," I said, my voice cracking like an adoles-
cent boy's.

"You're a fine-looking young man," she said. "You hardly look like
Percy at all, for which you should count yourself fortunate indeed."
She burst out laughing at her own joke, as did Judith. I had completely
forgotten Judith was in the room. Ciara was the sort of woman who
makes you forget others are in the room.

"I have so many things I'd like to ask you," I said.

"Then you're going to have to buy me a drink," Ciara said. "At the
very least."

"How about dinner?"

"Lovely, when?"

"How about now?"

Ciara batted her eyes. On another woman the gesture may have
seemed out of place, even desperate. But not on Ciara. She was so
beautiful it almost hurt to look. "Well then," she said. "Follow me."
Without another word she was out the door, leaving the bell jingling
in her wake. For a moment I couldn't move; I was simply overwhelmed.

From behind me, Judith cleared her throat. "It was delightful
meeting you," she said. "You'd best run along after her."

I turned in surprise. I had forgotten Judith again.

"Don't feel bad," she said. "Ciara has that effect on everyone. Just
shake my hand and walk out the door. Everything will be all right."

She extended her tiny hand. I grasped it loosely and smiled. Then

I took one last, deep breath before I chased my father's fifth wife out the door into the London night.

WE WERE STILL NEAR enough to the flower shop to smell the cigarettes outside the pub when Ciara stopped abruptly and pointed down an alley.

"That's where I live," she said. "Your father loved it."

"My father lived here?"

"Not exactly. He lived in Washington and New York. But he loved London and when he was here, this is where we stayed. Private Mews, flat fifteen, Kinnerton Place South."

"You lived here when you two were married?" I asked.

"Before, during, and after," she said. "I've had this flat thirty years, and I ain't going anywhere."

We continued walking. On Sloane Street, with the Knightsbridge Underground station in the foreground, we arrived at the place that had made Ciara famous. "Home away from home," she said, brushing her fingers gently against the glass door. "Harvey Nichols."

The department store, of which I'd heard but to which I'd never been, was as spectacular as advertised. Tall and stunning, with sensational windows, all the displays designed by Ciara herself: the Irish supermodel who'd been synonymous with the store long before she married the senator from America.

"Your father had a very sensitive eye when it came to fashion," she said.

That didn't seem to fit. "That surprises me," I said.

"It surprised me too," Ciara said. "I remember the first time we stood in this very spot, staring into this very same window. There was a tiny cat in the corner of the display, almost an afterthought. Percy took it all in quietly, then he turned to me and said: 'I think the cat should be on the bed.' And I asked him why, and he said: 'The colors are off. The cat is so light brown it is practically orange. Either put it on the bed, or get a darker cat.' You could have knocked me down with a feather, because he was absolutely right."

"What did you do?"

"I slept with him that night," she said with a devilish grin, "and the next day I changed the cat."

THE RESTAURANT, ZUMA, WAS on Raphael Street, a few short blocks away from the bustle.

We received a celebrity's greeting from the hostess and even more enthusiastic welcome from the flamboyant waiter, who appeared at our table the moment we were seated. "Delightful to see you, Ms. Cavanaugh," he said in an Irish accent nearly identical to hers. "How long has it been?"

"What time is it now?" she asked, and they laughed in unison. To me, she said: "I had lunch here, as I do nearly every day. Martin was here as well."

"As I am nearly every day," said Martin, and they laughed again. "What can I get for you to wet the whistle tonight?" he asked me, his hand absently resting on Ciara's shoulder.

"Whatever is the lady's pleasure, please bring two."

Without even asking he was gone, and Ciara settled comfortably into her chair. The room was dimly lit; a candle flickered on the table between us, reflecting in her eyes. "Tell me about yourself, Johnny," she said.

It made me think of Bruce, who was the only person who called me Johnny. "I grew up in New York," I said. "My mother was Percy's first wife."

"Alice, I know. Is she well?"

"She is, thank you."

"I'm delighted to hear that. I never met her, but I heard wonderful things about her. You should know that down deep inside, your father loved her to his dying day."

"Do you mean that?" I asked.

"I never say anything I don't mean."

That made me feel good. "I'll remember that," I said.

"What else?" she asked. "You married? Family?"

"Yes, I have two kids," I said. "And my wife is actually of Irish descent, named Claire."

"Lovely name."

"Where in Ireland are you from?" I asked.

"Limerick," she said proudly. "Have you heard of it?"

"Frank McCourt?"

"Precisely. I never met him. He made a lot of folks angry with his depiction but I found it mostly accurate. I was raised working-class, as he was. My father was conductor of the *Shannon Breeze*, the ferry that crosses right at the mouth of the river Shannon, from County Kerry to County Clare."

"Sounds exciting."

She eyed me like I had to be insane. "You're obviously a wealthy American," she said. "They were the only ones I ever saw smiling. Drove their cars onto the boat to cross over to play golf at Lahinch after playing Ballybunion. The Irish on the boat were freezing and miserable. The wind was so strong off the Atlantic, if you were on the deck you felt like you could be blown off. The air was always dank, fog over the water, wet even when it didn't rain."

The waiter returned, noisily, carrying two steaming ceramic flasks on a tray. He set them down in the center of the table, laid two small cups beside them.

"Do you like sake?" Ciara asked me.

For all my travels, and all my drinking, I'd never tried it. "I guess we're going to find out," I said, and poured two cups full to the rims and handed her one. We clinked. "To your health."

"Or yours," she said, "if you've never tried this before."

I enjoyed the sake a great deal; in fact I fired down two cupfuls as though they were shots, just as Ciara demonstrated. The flavor was bitter with a hint of fruit, more akin to beer than wine. The first shot warmed my chest. The second left the impression it could take any situation and make it better.

"So, how did you get from the deck of the ferry to London?" I asked.

Ciara put her hand to her chin thoughtfully. "I left school when I was sixteen. I had an older cousin who'd come to London to model; I stayed with her. She worked at the perfume counter at Harvey Nichols. My first day in town I cried from morning to night, homesick. My second day I went to visit my cousin at work. One of the designers was in the store that day, saw me. That fall I was on the cover of the catalog. That was forty years ago and I've been there ever since. No matter where my life has taken me, I've never left Harvey Nichols and I never will."

"Amazing story."

"All stories are amazing, Johnny. You just have to know how to tell them." She filled our cups again and, this time, sipped at the warm sake. I did too, and found I liked it less that way.

"Do you eat sushi?" Ciara asked.

"Love it."

"Perfect," she said, and raised her hand in the direction of the waiter. "Tell Eric to send out whatever suits him tonight."

Martin nodded and was gone as quickly as he'd come. I stared at Ciara, a little tipsy, so overcome by her I had no idea where to begin.

She did. "So, what would you like me to tell you?"

"You were with my father later in his life. What was it like?"

Ciara sighed deeply. "The truth, Johnny, is that it was awful." She looked at me with sad eyes. "I assume you want the truth."

I wasn't expecting that. I leaned closer. "Of course I do."

"When I met your father, his health was declining. He wasn't ill, per se, but he had everything wrong with him. Heart trouble, mostly, which caused a variety of problems."

"How was his mind?"

"Brilliant. He was the most brilliant man I ever met; no one else was close. But he was depressed. He hated growing old, Johnny. He used to beg me to make him young again."

"How?"

Ciara smiled. "Precisely."

I hadn't even noticed Martin approaching, but now he laid multiple dishes on the table: a plate of squid, another of eggplant, a tray of sushi rolls. It looked extraordinary, but I wasn't especially hungry. "Tell me more," I said.

"Your father was an obsessive person. He could be charming, but mostly he was manic. He could not sit still, ever. I would find him pacing during the night, physically exhausted but unable to rest. He would read three or four books in a week. It was as though he was an hour from death and wasn't going to waste a second."

"That's similar to what Anne told me. Sounds like it got worse."

"*Much*," Ciara said emphatically. "It got much worse."

"What did you do?"

"There wasn't anything to do. Your father married me because he thought I would make him feel vibrant again. Once he realized I couldn't, he didn't have much use for me at all. He wanted to talk about policy and government. I don't know a thing about those. I love things of beauty. He did too, but gradually those began to matter less and less, as though they were a waste of time."

"This was the same man who noticed the orange cat in the display?"

She shook her head. "He wasn't. That man slowly disappeared."

This was so far from the image I always had of my father. "So what happened?" I asked.

Ciara sighed. "I was smart in that I never let go the flat in London. I began spending more and more time here until it became obvious to us both we were married in name only."

"That reminds me," I said. "The other women my father married all took his name, and they all told me it was very important to him that they did. Why didn't you?"

The sparkle returned to her eyes. "Because, young man, when you are Ciara Cavanaugh you stay that way."

Her smile brightened my mood. I picked up a pair of chopsticks and speared a sushi roll, doused it in soy sauce, popped it in my mouth. "Delicious," I said.

"The best sushi in London."

Suddenly, I was hungry. I sampled the eggplant, which was equally superb.

"*Bon appétit,*" Ciara said.

I nodded politely, then motioned for the waiter. "This," I said to them both, "requires a bottle of wine. Lady's choice."

And so went our evening, a delightful hour of food and drink and conversation. Almost none of the rest of it involved Percy and that was fine by me; I had spent more than enough time thinking of my father. Ciara, meanwhile, was everything I imagined she would be: intelligent, fearless, provocative. I reveled in the opportunity to enjoy her company and ignore for a while the cloud that had been hovering over me.

When we were finished and back on the street she unsnapped her clutch and, to my surprise, retrieved a lighter and two cigarettes. She lit one and offered the second to me.

"Thanks, no," I said.

"Why don't Americans smoke anymore?" she asked.

"It's bad for your health."

"I know, but, Johnny, how long do you plan to live?"

"As long as I can."

Ciara sniffed dismissively. "Just like your father." She pointed her finger at my nose. "Don't be so afraid to die that you forget how to live, Johnny. *That's* what Percy did." Then she smiled. "Fancy a stroll? It's still early."

"I'd love it."

We started back in the direction from which we'd originally come, walking slowly and mostly in quiet. She pointed out a pub she liked, a shop where they sold the finest tea, the most overrated restaurant in Knightsbridge.

"Are you comfortable in silence?" I asked as we neared my hotel.

"Sorry?"

"It just reminds me of my mother, how you can be with someone and not feel compelled to fill the space with words. You and I are practically strangers, yet you seem content to be quiet."

"There isn't always something worth saying."

"I know," I said. "But that usually doesn't keep me from saying it."

"That doesn't tell me you're uncomfortable with me, it tells me you're uncomfortable with you."

I stopped short. I had never thought of it that way before.

"I didn't mean to insult you," she said. "Your father never stopped talking either; there was never a moment of silence with him."

"I'm not insulted," I said truthfully. "Was that a problem? That he was always talking?"

"In his very unique case, no. Because, bless him, he always had something interesting to say."

"What would he have said right now?"

Ciara looked me up and down. "He'd have said, 'Don't answer that, Cee, it's a trick question.'"

I laughed. We had reached my hotel but I wasn't ready for our time together to end. "I would love to keep walking, if you would," I said.

"Ever seen Buckingham Palace?"

"Only on television."

"Let's go."

It wasn't more than fifteen minutes' walk before we turned a corner and my breath caught in my throat. Before us, lit against the dark night, surrounded by uniformed guards and tourists of every nationality, was the palace. I had been to London on business a dozen times, but I had never been here. We walked closer, slowly, in unspoken reverence.

"Spectacular," I said.

"It is. No matter how you feel about the royals, the sight of it never grows old."

"Did my father like it?"

"Your father had business inside. He went in and out in the back of a limousine and, to my knowledge, never once looked out the window. Which is why he never once thought to ask the question you're about to ask me."

There wasn't any way not to be confused. "What?"

Ciara smiled devilishly. "Your father was always so busy looking ahead that he never looked around. I want *you* to look around right now, and ask me about the place where we are."

"Do you mean the palace?" I asked.

Ciara shook her head emphatically. "The palace is in *front* of us. Look around us."

We were standing in a grass field, lovely but not especially noteworthy. Mature trees encircled us, no statues, no extravagant lights.

"What do you see?" Ciara asked me.

"Nothing. It's just green."

"Precisely. It's called Green Park. Now, what do you notice about it that is unusual?"

There wasn't anything out of the ordinary, even the landscaping. In fact, there wasn't any landscaping at all.

"There are no flowers," I said.

Ciara's face broke into a wide smile; she clapped her hands joyfully. "Very good, Johnny. Your father could have stood beside us until the end of time and not noticed that."

I felt a surge of pride. "Why aren't there any flowers?" I asked.

"Depends on which story you believe. One version says it's because this was once a graveyard for lepers, and it was believed the disease would rise through the ground and be spread via the flowers."

"What's the other version?"

Ciara took a deep breath. "In the seventeenth century, King Charles II used to pick flowers from this park to give to his mistresses.

His wife, the queen, discovered his infidelity and ordered that all the flowers be pulled up."

"Which version is true?" I asked.

"The truth, Johnny, is whatever you choose to believe."

"Did my father say that?"

Ciara shook her head. "Johnny, your father never said any such thing. In fact, he would have said just the opposite."

"Are you telling me to be more like him?"

Ciara reached out and touched my cheek. I think I saw tears forming in her eyes. "No, darling," she said. "I'm telling you to be less."

AS WE APPROACHED CIARA'S flat we passed the flower shop and I was reminded of something Judith had told me. "She says that you saved her life," I said, indicating the florist's sign. "What does she mean by that?"

Ciara rolled her eyes. "My word, she is *such* a drama queen."

"What happened?"

"I've been on Kinnerton Place for thirty years. Judith has been longer than that. I happened into her shop one day and fell in love. How can you help it? It's so beautiful. As I became better known and my life became more frazzled, Judith became my solitude. I joined her in the shop for tea at least once a week, more if I could. The colors inspired me and soothed my soul. Years later, when your father and I were making the final arrangements of our divorce, I told him I didn't want any of his money. I have my own. I asked only that he purchase the shop from the owner of the building and gift it to Judith. He did, and put it in my name. So, technically, I own the shop, but I've told Judith from the very first that she can do whatever she pleases with it so long as she never leaves. If I die before she does I've left it to her; if she goes first I'll leave it to her daughter. That shop will be on that spot as long as I live, which means I will always have my sanity. And it's your father I have to thank for that."

I choked up. It was the first time in my entire life that I felt proud to be my father's son. "I want you to know," I said, "that of all the things anyone has told me about Percy, that was the only one that made me feel good."

I kissed her on both cheeks as we arrived at the entrance to the Private Mews where she lived, a few paces past the florist, on the other side of the pub where the crowd was still outside smoking.

"You are a lovely man," she said. "He missed out a lot when it came to you."

"I guess we both did."

"Perhaps," she said, "but he more than you."

Then she kissed me again, just brushing my lips with hers, and without another word strode quickly into the darkness that enveloped whatever was on the other side of the wall, while I struggled to keep from being knocked to the ground by the sheer force of her gentle touch.

THURSDAY

THE EIGHT O'CLOCK BRITISH Airways to JFK would have me in the office by noon, which was comfortably before Bruce's stern invitation for one o'clock. Thus, I found the travel relaxing and productive; I accomplished more during those seven hours than I had in the previous ten days combined.

In fact, I spent almost no time thinking about Percy. Only once did he cross my mind and even that came with a smile. It was when I first opened my briefcase and found Judith Blacklock's floral curriculum, detailing a variety of courses and diplomas as well as tips for floral arrangements and payment plans for students. The thought of Judith surreptitiously sneaking a brochure into my briefcase while I was distracted by Ciara made me laugh out loud.

Sonny pulled up outside our midtown office building at five minutes past noon. I was feeling jaunty and relieved as I approached the revolving doors on Sixth Avenue, briefcase in one hand, garment bag slung over the other shoulder; it was good to be back. My travels had begun to feel like an odyssey; I needed some time to digest all I had discovered and figure out what it meant. Meanwhile, I was just looking forward to being in my office, perhaps even basketball later in the day.

As I stepped toward the building I saw a man beside the entrance who appeared out of place. He was tall and thin with a mustache, wearing a Yankees cap and denim jacket. There was something startlingly familiar about his face, mostly the mustache. The man was also obviously drawn to me, staring directly into my eyes, nodding just enough to make it clear he was seeking my attention.

I approached with a quiver in my belly. "Can I help you?" I asked.

The instant he began to speak I recognized the face surrounding the mustache. "Mr. Sweetwater, would you be able to take a quick stroll around the block with me?" He began to walk and I fell in alongside, striding quickly to keep pace with his long legs. He walked like a man determined not to let anyone notice that his mustache did not belong on his face. "Why have you not replied to my e-mails?" he asked.

"What?"

"As I detailed for you in my office, I sent you an e-mail Monday, a second Tuesday, a third yesterday, from the account of an insurance agent soliciting your business."

"I didn't get them," I said.

"I know you've been traveling but you were here for portions of Monday and Tuesday," he said, a hint of frustration in his tone. "I assume you have the ability to receive e-mail when you are not in your office. Could they have been rejected by corporate firewalls?"

"I can't imagine. We have the worst tech security in the world. I just sent a note complaining about it last week."

"That could explain it. You're a powerful executive; I assume your complaints are met with hasty action. In this case, that action seems to have derailed our plans. But only temporarily."

I felt myself shudder with realization about the e-mail. Not the ones I hadn't received from Cranston. The one I hadn't received from Claire.

Cranston was walking so fast it was difficult to keep pace. "So," he said, "are you prepared to receive my report?"

Quickly, I stopped thinking about the e-mails. I stopped walking also, abruptly and without consideration. The question should not have taken me by surprise, but still I was fully unprepared to answer. I merely watched as Cranston continued up Sixth Avenue, turned the corner onto Forty-eighth Street, disappeared from sight.

A garbage truck was blocking two lanes of traffic, which caused every taxi driver to lean on his horn and shout expletives out the window. On the sidewalk, men in suits and women in heels and a guy pushing a laundry cart stepped around me; some paused to glare. I still didn't move. I just waited and watched the corner, where eventually Cranston appeared again and leaned against the side of the building, talking into a cell phone.

The first step I took in his direction felt monumental, like Neil Armstrong on the moon. The second came more easily, the third easier still. I was striding at a normal pace as I approached the corner and turned, right in front of Cranston, who waited a beat before following. "There is no rush," he said as he pulled even. "You can take all the time you need."

"Can I ask you something?" I said, my anxiety mounting. "Do I *want* this information?"

This time it was Cranston who stopped dead in his tracks. "I have no way of answering that question," he said, a touch of sympathy in his voice. "I have information that is significant only because you hired me to do this job. If you don't want to know, then it is of no significance at all. It can be easily discarded and no one will ever know a thing." There was nothing in his face or tone that indicated what he knew.

"I have to be at a meeting in a few minutes," I said. "I can't make this decision right now."

"Then don't." Cranston took the phone he'd been pretending to use, touched the screen, handed it to me. "I will call you on this line tomorrow afternoon. The phone has been programmed to accept calls from only one source, so if someone else dials the number accidentally it will not be received. The phone will make no sound, it will only vibrate, so if you are in a position where you cannot respond merely ignore the vibration. Do not attempt to return the call, I will try again five minutes after the first time and then every five minutes until you answer. Do you understand?"

I nodded.

Cranston smiled. "It was a pleasure chatting with you," he said. "I trust our paths will cross again."

He turned and crossed the street behind him, stepping between two cabs at a red light. I stared at the phone in my hand for a moment, then tucked it into my breast pocket and started back. It was nearly one o'clock.

IN MY OFFICE, I stared at photos of the kids. Tonight was their school concert. I wouldn't miss that for anything. I had a father who missed school concerts; I would never be one. I was thinking, too, of Claire. I felt like so much had changed in eleven days, but the one thing that hadn't was whatever happened in my guest room.

Cranston knew. Whatever it was, he knew it and was prepared to deliver it as soon as I was prepared to receive it. That was the easy part. The tricky part would be what came next. If Cranston presented me with evidence that Claire was having an affair, what then? I would confront her with what I'd seen, of course, but then what? Storm angrily out the door? Headed where? My entire life has been spent trying to find the exact place I am in today. From the smell of fresh dill in the hallway of my father's building to the clicks and clacks of my mother's doors, to the gentle way Claire rests her hand in the center of my chest when she falls asleep. Where would the next stop be? An apartment in the city? My kids every other weekend? Evenings in clubs with cocaine-snorting models or disenchanted girls with pierced tongues? I wasn't interested in that life *before* I was married. I certainly wasn't interested now. So, in truth it really wasn't the pending call from Cranston that worried me. It was what I would need to do after I hung up the phone.

There was a knock on my door promptly at one o'clock. It was Bruce, tie loosened, the smile of an expectant father on his lips. "In the gym," he said. "Five minutes to change clothes."

I was in the elevator four minutes later, wearing Under Armour and Air Jordans, and I was confused. As much as Bruce loves basketball, this hardly met the level of urgency I was anticipating. Bruce is well aware that when he sends a message his demand will come before any and all others; family and business considerations will be overlooked, consequences ignored. For all he knew, I could be closing a deal worth a billion dollars. To call me in for a game of basketball was highly unusual.

Then the elevator doors parted on the nineteenth floor, and just like that it made all the sense in the world. Stepping into the gym I felt a surge of adrenaline. Sweat broke out at my hairline; my breath came quickly. I put my hand out as he approached, bigger than life, bigger than even in my wildest imagination.

"Jonathan Sweetwater," Bruce said. "Say hello to Michael Jordan."

We shook hands. His were damp with perspiration. Or perhaps those were mine; it wasn't clear.

"Nice shoes," he said, looking down at my feet.

"Thanks," I said. "I never play without them."

Jordan nodded. "Neither do I."

Bruce shoved a basketball into the center of my chest. "Warm up, we don't have all day. I told Michael you're going to kick his ass. And you better, or the whole deal he's making with us is off."

I was so taken aback, I needed the smile on Jordan's face to realize that was a joke. But we *were* going to play. I started to dribble. Right hand, left hand, between the legs, jump shot.

Jordan nodded. "Looks good."

"I told you," Bruce said. "He's going to kick your ass."

I took a few more jump shots, then sprinted the length of the court twice. A drop of sweat rolled down my cheek to my jaw. "I'm ready," I said.

Jordan turned and heaved a ball one-handed toward the basket on the opposite end of the court. It banked hard off the backboard and straight through the hoop, barely disturbing the net before crashing to the floor. "I didn't call that off the glass," he said. "Your ball."

Bruce tossed me a basketball and stepped away backward, taking a seat on the wooden bench. I stood a moment, mesmerized, the leather in my hands, the wood of the floor, the beating of my heart. With no further consideration, I began to dribble. I went to my right because I always begin to my right; most defenders assume I can only drive to my dominant side, so I take them to the right, then surprise them with a quick move back the other way.

Jordan met me as I crossed the middle of the court and put his hand in the small of my back. "Any time you want, make that move left," he said, under his breath but loud enough that he meant for me to hear. "All you Wall Street guys have that same move."

It was surreal and exciting to have Michael Jordan talking trash to me. The trouble was he had anticipated the only move I have. Flustered, I backed away. Then, staring right in his face, I rose up and tried a long jump shot.

The ball seemed to remain in the air forever. I could see it rotate in slow motion, as though my entire life—or at least the last eleven days—had been spent in pursuit of this moment, this one chance for unfathomable glory. It was a longer shot than I generally take, but my energy level was raised so high I knew it would reach the rim. The arc was perfect; I could tell as it flew that it had a chance.

Swish!

A burst of energy raced through me as Jordan retrieved the ball. Bruce was cheering wildly from the sideline. Jordan advanced toward me, his signature tongue hanging out the side of his mouth. "Which way do you want me to take you?" he asked.

I lowered into my defensive posture, eyes locked. "I'm ready either way."

Jordan turned and backed into me. I shoved with everything I had to keep from retreating. "Watch out now," he whispered, "here it comes."

I stepped backward, leaving plenty of space between us. Jordan turned as well, so we were squared up, knees bent, sweat dripping.

"You don't have this shot," I said.

Jordan's eyes narrowed, and in a flash he elevated, so quickly I had no chance to do anything but turn and watch the ball as it left his fingers and sailed toward the basket, climbing in a perfect arc, then diving toward the hoop. I held my breath.

Clang!

Jordan's shot hit hard off the back of the rim and bounced skyward, back toward where we stood. The backboard was quivering, as though it knew this was no ordinary shot it had rejected.

Bruce was making enough noise for ten people. The ball bounced directly into my hands and instinct took over. I spun to my left and raced up the court as fast as I had ever run in my life. I could hear distant footsteps behind me but my path to the basket was clear. On the final step I gathered myself and lifted off my right foot, sailing toward the rim, the ball extended in my left hand, ready to gently kiss it off the glass for an easy basket.

Thwack!

I never saw him coming. I'm not even sure which side he came from, all I knew was he suddenly appeared before me as though he'd materialized from thin air. Jordan didn't block my shot so much as he caught it, loudly. Then, without slowing, he circled and headed off in the other direction. I tried to spin as well but my feet would have none of it. I crashed to the ground in a heap, lifting my head just in time to see Jordan's monster dunk at the other end.

"Your ball," he said as he jogged back toward me.

I pushed myself off the ground and raced past him to retrieve the ball, which had rolled into a corner and come to rest a few feet from where Bruce was seated. "That was something else," Bruce said.

We played for the better part of an hour and I did not score again. I lost track of exactly how many baskets Jordan made, somewhere between sixty and eighty, but I never gave up the fight, and when finally Bruce began applauding and came walking toward us I was beaming with pride.

"How about this kid, Mike?" he asked.

Jordan nodded. "You were right," he said. "He can play."

Bruce put a hand on my shoulder. "Take a shower, I'll bring Mike down to your office in a little while."

I looked Jordan directly in the eye once more and nodded, and he nodded back, with a level of respect that was—to me—too significant for words. I still had the ball in my hands as I watched them step into the elevator and the doors slide shut. I paused a moment, trying to grasp what had happened, but that wasn't remotely possible. Instead, one more time I tried my most familiar move, the fake to the right and then hard drive left. I pulled up a few feet from the hoop and banked a shot in off the backboard. Then I walked straight to the showers, peeling my soaked shirt over my head, listening as the ball bounced away behind me amid the enthusiastic cheers of an imaginary crowd offering a well-deserved standing ovation.

WORD THAT MICHAEL JORDAN was in the building spread like wildfire. By the time I stepped off the elevator to return to my office the floor was flooded with faces. Most people knew Bruce and I were basketball buddies; they likely figured mine would be an office Jordan might visit. There were more people on the floor than actually worked at our firm; I didn't recognize everyone.

Among the faces I did know was that of Ken Siegel, a senior executive responsible for all our corporate security, including digital. I wouldn't have taken him for a sports fan. He seemed more the artsy type, always wearing a neatly knotted bow tie and matching pocket square. The sight of him made the image of Cranston and his fake mustache pop into my head. It raised a question, and Ken was just the person to answer.

I stopped by his side as I made my way through the crowd. "Ken, do you have a minute?"

Despite his high standing in the company, the look on his face was as though he had just won the lottery. I felt all eyes on us as we made our way into my office and shut the door behind.

"Quick question," I said when he was seated opposite my desk, "if you aren't in a hurry to be anywhere."

"I have plenty of time," Ken said, smiling.

"I recall sending you a note last week about firewalls."

"Of course, and I appreciate it. I put my two best techs on it and we found a few areas we could tighten up. They were here all weekend and we instituted the changes Monday morning. Are you still having issues with spam?"

"Absolutely not. You did a terrific job, I commend you."

"It's my staff that deserves the credit."

"Then I commend them," I said. "I'm curious about something. Is it possible to view mail that gets denied?"

"Of course. Is there something in particular you were expecting?"

I didn't want to raise suspicion. "No, I was just wondering, as I have noticed a reduction in the flow and I was concerned that my moment of frustration last week might create problems down the road." Needlessly wordy. All the better to keep Ken from asking questions.

"No problem," he said, and came over to my side of the desk. "Let me show you." He made a few clicks with the mouse and a moment later a new folder appeared on my screen. "I'll title this 'junk' for you. You can change that to whatever you want. Anything that gets blocked by our filters will appear here. That doesn't include attachments that are deemed dangerous by our system; I can't authorize access to those."

"No problem."

Ken went back around the desk. "How's the family?" he asked, dropping into a chair.

"Healthy and happy," I said. "You?"

"Fine," he said. "My kid is very into sports. Not really my thing, but when he heard Jordan was here he about lost his mind. Begged his mother to take him out of school and bring him down."

"And?"

"They should be here any minute."

"So you're feeling some pressure."

"You better believe it."

I smiled. There was something delightful about the whole thing. Meanwhile, I had a question and this was the time to ask it.

"Ken," I said softly, "you can stay here as long as you like. Jordan will be here for sure. I don't know when, but Bruce told me they'd stop by. Have your wife and son come directly here and I'll make sure they meet him."

The joy was evident on Ken's face. "Thank you," he said.

"But I have something I need to ask in return," I said. "And this has to stay strictly between us."

Ken was unfazed, probably because he was too excited about introducing his son to Michael Jordan to be worried about anything.

I glanced at the computer screen on my desk. The file titled "junk" was open, and what appeared to be hundreds of e-mails were trapped in its purgatory. I went to the search function and typed in the letters "Cr." Instantly, three e-mails materialized, sent by "Cranston and Associates." I didn't need to open any of them. I knew what they'd say.

And then I saw, above Cranston's three e-mails, one from Claire.

Subject: last night!, with eleven photos attached. The pictures must have activated the firewall. I felt a tiny muscle deep inside of me unclench. It was one of those like a refrigerator humming, where you don't notice until it ceases. I hadn't realized it had been clenched until now that it was not. It felt good.

"Ken, how many people do we have in corporate security?" I asked.

"Full time, two dozen," he said, still at ease.

"How many of those are assigned to computer stuff, like viruses?"

"Most of them. Viruses and digital espionage are the twenty-first-century corporate concerns. People aren't going to break into your office to steal your secrets anymore, they're going to break into your computer."

"I understand." I drummed my fingers on the desk. "Ken, do you remember Reggie Fernandez?"

The expression on his face grew more serious. "Of course."

"He worked on my team. I know most of what went on, and I'm not asking you to tell me anything I'm not supposed to know. My question is, are matters of that sort handled by your department?"

Ken shifted uncomfortably in his chair. "On the record, the answer to that question is yes."

"How about off the record?"

Ken leaned closer to me, lowered his voice. "We handle all the paperwork. But I think what you're asking is if we handled the part of the investigation that led to his somewhat surprising departure?"

I nodded.

Ken breathed a heavy sigh. "Jon, I could lose my job for this."

"No one will ever know," I said.

Ken's face was deadly serious. "Bruce has outside assistance for matters such as those," he whispered. "I don't have any idea how it is accounted for procedurally, but the work is not done by any of our people."

"Who does it?"

"I'm sorry, I can't say any more."

I leaned closer. "Ken, I understand your obligations, but I have more at stake here than I can explain to you. It has nothing to do with the company. This is strictly personal. You have my word it will *never* come back to you."

Ken was pale now, fidgeting in his seat. "I want to help, Jon, I do. But . . ."

I came around the desk and knelt by his chair. I didn't know if there could be any recording devices in the room. Ken probably did know but I wasn't going to ask; I was just going to whisper directly into his ear, softly enough that no one else could possibly hear. "Let me do this: I will say a name, and all you have to do is give me a clear indication of whether I have the right person or not. Is that acceptable?"

"Go ahead."

"Lowell Cranston," I whispered.

Very slowly, Ken closed his eyes and shook his head from side to side.

"You're saying no?" I whispered.

"That is what I'm saying."

"Are you familiar with that name?"

"I am," he said, so quietly I had to strain to hear, "but that is not who handled the matter you asked me about."

I rested my elbow on my knee. Now to the thought I'd had in the hall. "Is the one who handled it an older man? White hair, white beard, fancy dresser, probably close to seventy?"

This time, unmistakably, Ken nodded his head up and down.

Before I could ask anything else, my intercom sounded and my assistant's loud voice shattered the quiet. "Mr. Siegel's wife and son are here," she said.

I stood up and straightened my trousers. Ken put his finger to his lips, and I nodded my assurance. Then I went back around behind my desk, dragged Claire's email with the photos into my regular inbox, and with an anxious smile shouted into the intercom. "Please bring them in!"

TWO HOURS LATER, PROMPTLY at five o'clock, my phone buzzed in my pocket just as I settled into the back of Sonny's car. Without looking I knew it was Claire, calling to remind me of the concert.

"A step ahead of you," I said as I answered. "Already in the car."

"How about a hello?" She sounded a bit put off.

"Hello," I said. "I'm on my way to school."

"What's with the attitude?" she asked. "Everything all right at the office? How was London? You never called."

She was right. It was the first time in all the years we had been married, through all my travels, that I had failed to at least send her a text. That hadn't occurred to me until she mentioned it. She was right to be put off. "I'm sorry," I said. "Just so busy, and exhausted. Too much travel, not enough sleep. I'm going to shut my eyes and I'll be good as new when I get there."

Claire waited a moment before softening. "Well, I missed you," she said. "I'll see you at school, we'll meet in the parking lot."

I clicked the phone off and then turned it off. I needed a few unobstructed minutes. With my eyes shut, I leaned more deeply into the plush leather seat. Truthfully, it was delightful to hear her voice. Even after all these years, it still cheered and soothed me. If only there wasn't all this other mess to consider. Life was so much easier when there wasn't any mess.

The image of the older man in Bruce's car entered my thoughts. I hadn't given him much consideration during that night; the whole event had been so surreal he had faded into the background. I hadn't thought of him again until this day, but now that I had it was clear his presence was the only one that hadn't fit. It still didn't.

Unless he was there because of me. Was that possible? Did Bruce want incriminating evidence against me? If so, for what reason? Had I done something wrong?

After a few minutes, the steady rhythm of the tires on the blacktop began to infiltrate my brain. I could feel myself slipping away. I kicked off my shoes and allowed myself to drift. Perhaps some sleep really was what I needed. There wasn't anything I had to know that wouldn't wait at least until I got to school.

I slept hard and woke with a jolt when the car came to a sudden stop.

"Sorry, sir," Sonny said in his heavy accent. "We're here."

Eleven days of nonstop time zone change had finally caught up to me. My head was heavy and dark. I pushed open the car door and nearly fell into the cool evening air.

"Have a good night," I said to Sonny. "Thanks."

I shook my head, trying to clear the cobwebs, and stumbled to the bench by the playground, the same bench where I'd sat with Betsy two days before. The breeze was helping to restore my head. I dug around in my briefcase and found two after-dinner mints, which I popped quickly into my mouth. The sugar helped stimulate my mind and I thought of Ciara, who'd grabbed a handful of the mints from a bowl at the host stand as we left the restaurant. Could that really have been only yesterday?

I took my phone from my breast pocket and opened the e-mail from Claire. There were eleven attachments. As I waited for them to download I let my head roll back and enjoyed the sun on my face, those delightful final rays before sunset, glowing and warm.

The phone vibrated in my hand. I looked down and scrolled slowly through the pictures. Claire and I coming through the revolving door, that fleeting instant before the surprise. The expression on my face when I realized. Me on my knees with the kids' faces buried into my sides. Claire and the kids, smiling for the camera. Phoebe and her best friend, Macy, hugging with exaggerated smiles. Macy is Betsy's daughter; the next picture was of the three of them—Phoebe and Macy with

Betsy between, all of them beaming. I looked deeply into Betsy's smile, using my thumb and forefinger on the screen to enlarge her face, until the two girls disappeared and it was only Betsy, her dark hair flowing, so much like Claire's. Her eyes were wide, her teeth stunningly white. Betsy looked perfect, and yet there was something in the photo that didn't sit right. I stared in silence, breathing deeply. Shut my eyes, opened them again. I couldn't pinpoint what was askew, and yet I was absolutely certain something was.

Meanwhile, cars were beginning to arrive in the parking lot behind me. I recognized several of the faces as they piled out: teachers, parents, little boys with their usually unruly hair combed neatly, little girls in bright-colored dresses, ribbons in their hair. I saw Claire's car pull in behind the bench. The rear door opened and both my kids popped out. Phoebe never even looked in my direction, she just headed straight into the building, but Drew saw me and came running at top speed as Claire pulled away to find parking. I went to my knees and he dove into me, reckless and trusting, as certain as he could be that his father would catch him. I hugged him tight, turned him upside down, and dangled him by his feet.

"Tummy! Tummy!" he yelled, his shirttail covering his face. His bare tummy was too inviting not to tickle. "Tummy!" he yelled again, louder this time.

I bent down and grabbed his hands with the one I had free, pulled him so he was right-side up, and dropped him softly onto his feet.

"Again!" he yelled.

I laughed. "Not now, we don't have enough time," I said. "We need to get you inside to sing." I took him by the hand and we began to walk toward the school. The sun was setting over the top of the building, casting long shadows all around us. Drew was humming. I couldn't make out the tune, if there was one at all. I looked down at his face and watched as he passed through the shadows into the sun, then the shadows, then the sun, and every time he emerged into the light he wrinkled his nose and squinted as his too-long hair flopped over his forehead.

Then I stopped walking, more abruptly than I meant to because Drew's arm jerked backward and he fell into me. I crouched down to his height, our faces inches apart. "Buddy," I said, "I hope you love this place as much as I do. It's such a beautiful place."

Drew looked around. "Dad," he said hesitantly, "it's school."

"I *know* it is," I said, "but it's a beautiful place. You always have to be somewhere; this is a wonderful place to have to be. Do you understand what I mean?"

He nodded slowly. Despite the fact there was no way he understood what I meant, because even I didn't understand what I meant.

I dropped Drew off in his classroom and hurried to the gymnasium, where about a hundred folding chairs had been opened in two long rows. It's always a race to get seats for the concerts because there are more parents and grandparents and sisters and brothers than there are chairs, so half the room winds up standing. Experienced parents have a plan; in our case, Claire parks the car, and I grab the two best seats I can find, sit in one, and place my briefcase on the other. This time I got hugely lucky: two prime seats were available, third row, center. I settled in, took a deep breath, and looked around. I saw my friend Scott Edwards two rows away, energy trader, smart as a whip. Next to him John Severin, older, probably sixty, on his second wife who isn't a whole lot older than the kids he has from his first. Jon Biele in the row behind me, drinks as much as anyone I've ever known. I leaned back in my seat and took another deep breath: familiar place, familiar faces.

Then, from behind, I felt two hands cover my eyes, small with warm palms, slick with moisturizer. They smelled of pomegranate, and faintly of a perfume I have loved for years though I don't know the name.

"Guess who?"

I didn't have to guess. I just let her hands rest over my eyes, enjoyed the scent.

"How was London?" Claire asked, moving my briefcase and taking the seat beside mine.

Before I could answer, another face materialized as if from nowhere. It was Betsy, fully made up, hair done, dressed more for a dinner date than a school concert. "Evening, Jon," she said, her voice scratchy. "I wore your favorite jeans." They probably weren't even the same jeans she wore the night I fondled her; she says that all the time.

Claire was fiddling with her camera. The lights went down and applause began to ring across the room as the headmaster made his way toward the stage. Betsy wedged between Claire and me so we were all sharing two seats. She and Claire locked arms, Betsy's hand resting on Claire's thigh, her other in her own lap, trembling slightly. I closed my eyes as the applause settled and the headmaster welcomed us all to the lower-school concert. It felt good to close my eyes. The second graders were the first to take the stage. Drew's grade would be next; I had a moment to rest. A child's voice announced they would be singing "Hakuna Matata" and "World Without Love." As the singing started images began to swirl in my mind: Drew's face going in and out of the shadows, Phoebe letting go of my hand when her friends were nearby, Lowell Cranston with his feet up on a desk, the dapper man in the tuxedo on the sofa in Bruce's apartment. I cracked open an eye and looked down to see Betsy and Claire holding hands. Then the applause rose again, and Claire and Betsy together stood up.

"Doesn't he look *so* cute?" Claire whispered excitedly.

I stood as well and looked up to the stage. There was Andrew in the front row, his hair neatly combed, shirt buttoned all the way up.

"He's your mini-me, Jon!" said Betsy. There was a faint but clear whiff of alcohol on her breath.

Drew and his class were singing "Puff, the Magic Dragon," which usually makes me laugh, but I was too tired. It was all I could do just to listen.

Claire was beaming when the first graders shuffled off the stage. She scrolled through the pictures she had taken with her phone. "This one's good," she said to herself. "His eyes are closed in this one."

Then the fourth grade was marching in, which meant Phoebe, as well as Betsy's daughter, Macy. Betsy rose and leaned over to kiss Claire, her butt directly in my face. "I'm going down to the front to take pictures," she whispered.

Claire squeezed her arm. Betsy lingered in front of me a moment, then worked her way through the seated row to the aisle. I stood to allow her to pass and remained standing as I watched the kids file into place. Phoebe was on the second of three risers, all the way to the right side. Most of the kids were scanning the audience in search of their parents, but not my daughter. Phoebe was staring straight ahead, a confident smile on her face. She knew with absolute certainty her mother and father were out there beyond the lights. She didn't need to see us to be sure. With that thought, to my horror, a lump came up in my throat, large and with great force. I swallowed hard, desperate for a drink of water or anything else that might keep me from bursting into tears.

The teacher nodded to a boy named Aidan, who stepped forward to a microphone that was positioned a foot over his head. The teacher adjusted the mike downward, drawing a laugh.

"The fourth grade," Aidan announced, "will be singing 'All You Need Is Love,' a song made famous by a band from England called the Beatles."

Another ripple of laughter. There isn't anything in the world funnier than children when they aren't trying to be.

Then they began to sing the song. It wasn't perfect, but it was markedly better than I would have expected. I knew the song backward and forward; I couldn't count how many times as a child I listened to my mother sing it. And now here was Phoebe, wearing a lime-green dress, her eyes straight ahead, singing it confidently with a little smile on her face.

I felt a squeeze of my hand. I turned and found Claire staring right into my face, her eyes filled with tears. She leaned close and whispered, "I know how difficult it is for you with your dad. But *you* are the best father I could ever imagine." Then she squeezed my hand again and I squeezed back. As usual, she knew how I felt better than I did. And so we stayed that way for the rest of the performance, holding hands, both of us crying as we watched our daughter sing her grand-mother's favorite song.

THE CONCERT WAS A smashing success. All were delighted with the songs sung and photos taken and cupcakes eaten. When we arrived home, Claire suggested to both kids that they kiss me good night. "Daddy has been working *so* hard," she said. "He needs his sleep."

"I'm all right," I said to her privately. "I thought we'd sit up and have a drink after they hit the sack."

"No whispering!"

The children admonished us—we don't allow exclusionary discussion in the house. The kids aren't allowed to keep secrets from each other, so in their minds Claire and I should not be allowed either.

"Daddy gets to whisper," Claire told them. "When you are grown up you get to make the rules and then you get to break them." Then, under her breath, to me: "You've been exhausted. Get some sleep. I promised Betsy I would spend some time on the phone with her tonight."

"Why?"

Claire wrinkled her brow. "I assume you know they're going through some stuff."

"What does that have to do with you?"

"I am *there* for her," Claire said. "She's my friend."

I let it go at that. I kissed both children on top of their heads and Claire quickly on the lips, then I went up the stairs. I stopped at the top and looked left into my bedroom, then turned right and made my way, once again, down the hallway to the guest room. I turned on the lights. Everything was exactly as it should have been. There was no indication anyone had set foot in the room since I last had, two days before. I switched the light back off and shut the door behind me.

That door usually remains open, but for some reason I felt like closing it.

And that was when it hit me. In fact, it nearly ran me over, a burst
of cold electricity that began in my gut and spread until I could feel my
fingers tingling. Very slowly, standing in the exact space where it had
all begun, I reached into my breast pocket for my phone. The image
on the screen was as I had left it, Betsy Buchanan smiling, her daughter and mine eschewed by the manner in which I had enlarged the
face. My hands were shaking as I placed my thumb and forefinger
once more to the screen and then gingerly slid them together, watching as Betsy's features slid further away, then as Phoebe and Macy
appeared. My breath caught in my chest, literally, in the instant that I
realized what it was I had missed.

A few steps behind the three smiling faces, filling the space
between the top of Macy's head and her mother's shoulder, was a man.
His face was turned to the side and I didn't recognize it. But I would
never forget the ponytail. The man was wearing a pink, button-down
shirt, open at the collar with a pair of designer sunglasses hanging on
the shirt, beneath his chin. He did not appear to be talking to anyone.
Though I couldn't be certain, it seemed he was by himself, and it also
seemed he was glancing down at Betsy; in fact, as I looked more
closely, it seemed pretty clear that he was staring at her ass. "I get it,"
I said. And shut off the phone. Back in my bedroom I undressed and
left my clothes in a pile in the closet. I brushed my teeth and slid
between the crisply laid sheets, cool and soft. The image of Claire and
Betsy holding hands at the concert flashed before my eyes. I couldn't
recall ever seeing such closeness between them before. Had they
grown markedly closer in recent times? Why wouldn't I have known
that? I had so many questions, but in the end only one of them really
mattered. Was it possible that Betsy was the one having an affair? And
Claire knew the details, because she used our house? Was it possible
that it was actually Betsy, who is so much like Claire I had twice mistaken her, in our guest room that day?

Well, why would Betsy not use her own house? That answer came quickly. Her husband traveled all the time and she did not seem to have the most specific understanding of his plans; just this week she had told me she *thought* he was in Prague. I assume if you aren't certain if your husband is in Prague, you also aren't certain when he's coming home. Such uncertainty would have to make scheduling an extramarital tryst complicated.

That actually made some semblance of sense. More difficult to fathom was why Claire would allow Betsy to use our home. "I'm *there* for her," she had said. I wouldn't have expected Claire to facilitate anything like that, but then if there was one thing I had learned from all this it was that people are sometimes capable of things that surprise me.

With that I rolled onto my side, fluffed the pillows, and fell asleep with all the lights on. I never heard Claire come in, but when I awoke nine hours later she was snoring gently beside me.

FRIDAY

I FELT FRESH AND awake on the train in the morning, despite a gloomy sky. I proceeded to the gym, where I worked out hard on the treadmill, a little sore on my right hip where Jordan had inadvertently jabbed me with an elbow. I smiled at the thought. *Michael Jordan accidentally hurt me playing basketball.* Whatever else had come of the previous eleven days of my life, I would always have that.

I ate breakfast at my desk as I sifted through e-mail. I saw the file titled "junk" but did not open it. There wasn't any reason. I hadn't a need for a penile enlargement kit, and the phone Cranston had given me was in my pocket. I'd checked it twice already. There were no missed calls.

I was on the floor, stretching my back, reading the *Wall Street Journal*, when I heard a light tap at my door. I looked up expecting Bruce but instead found Ken, wearing a blue blazer with an orange bow tie and matching pocket square.

"Don't get up," he said as I did anyway. "Just wanted to say thanks again for yesterday. My son will never forget it. He made my wife print out copies of all the pictures he took so he could bring them to school. He's going to be the most popular kid in the lunchroom."

I smiled. "I think it was a thrill for all of us."

Ken gently shut the door behind him. His expression turned grim. "Jon, I didn't sleep for a second last night. I've been here twenty years. This company is my life. I will lose my job if you tell anyone about what we discussed or use the information in any way. You know that, don't you?"

I nodded.

"I have no idea what's going on and I'm sorry if you're mixed up in something, but I can't help, whatever it is. And I should never have gone as far as I did. I'm here to beg you, Jon, literally beg you. You met my wife, my son. They depend on me."

I pointed toward the chair opposite the desk, where he'd sat the day before. "Ken, I understand exactly what you're saying, and you have my word nothing will ever come back to you."

"Thank you," Ken said, and sat down, though he didn't look less worried. He looked like a man who believed he would have to be worried for the rest of his life.

"Ken, what does he want from me?" I asked.

Ken shook his head and raised both his hands, palms facing me. "I've said far more than I ever should have. I would help you any way I could, Jon. But I can't."

I leaned back in my chair. "How old are you, Ken?"

"Older than you think I am," he said. "I'll be fifty next year."

"I just turned forty."

"Happy birthday."

"Thanks," I said. "Tell me, does it ever slow down?"

"What?"

"Time," I said. "It's been moving real fast for me lately. I'm hoping it will slow down."

"I'm afraid it works the other way. Just gets faster and faster. I was forty a few weeks ago."

I nodded. "You don't have anything to worry about," I said. "I promise."

I saw genuine relief in his face, which made me feel good. Then the intercom buzzed on my desk. That would be Bruce. No one else would disturb me with my door shut. Bruce wouldn't wait long either; he never does. I rose from my chair, headed toward the door. As I passed Ken I stopped, knelt, put my face right by his ear.

"Listen to me," I whispered. "We have one minute and no more than that. Answer me *this* question: Are there microphones in here? Can anyone hear me right now besides you?"

Very deliberately, Ken shook his head side to side. The answer was no.

"That's what I thought," I said, no louder than before. "Then answer me one more question and you'll never hear from me again. You have my word this will never come back to you under any circumstances." Ken fidgeted. "You said yourself you've already gone farther than you should. Help me out with one more answer and that will be the end of it. Just tell me why he did it."

Ken turned and looked me square in the face. He sighed lightly. "Don't let it worry you. He does it with everyone. It doesn't mean he doesn't trust you or wants to get rid of you. It's just the way he is. That's how you get to be him, and stay him. If he ever needs anything on you, he has it. It's as simple as that. You can't take it personally. It isn't meant that way."

My hand was on Ken's shoulder; we were staring each other in the eye. There wasn't any question he was telling the truth. I nodded gently and patted him on the back. Then I went to the door, opened it, and told Bruce I'd be ready to play in five minutes.

BACK ON NINETEEN, I warmed up with jump shots. I felt good, my rhythm unstoppable, my technique impeccable. I wanted to play well. For the first time ever, it was important to me that I beat Bruce in basketball.

I felt betrayed, and confused, and a little bit sad. But if you added those together they wouldn't equal the power of my most overriding emotion: deflation. For the second time in as many weeks, I was wondering if a relationship I valued wasn't really what I believed it to be. I dribbled rapidly between my legs, behind my back, fired jump shot after jump shot. I was thinking of Percy. I have spent my entire life with the image of my father I had when I was nine years old. At that age, like most boys do, I looked up to him as a hero, if only because he was a man and I was a boy. It occurred to me that Bruce was right around the same age Percy was when I last saw him. And he was very much like my father, as best I could tell. I never really knew my father. I thought I knew Bruce. Maybe I didn't after all.

Bruce lumbered in a few minutes behind me, limping badly on his right side. "This damn calf is acting up."

"Won't stop you from kicking my ass," I said, trying to mask the conflict in my tone.

He snorted. "After what you did to Michael yesterday, I'm lucky if you'll play with me at all."

"He killed me."

"He's the greatest player that ever lived," Bruce said. "You did real good. He was impressed." I stopped shooting. Bruce tossed me a bottle of Gatorade. "I was too. You made me proud."

There was no mistaking the genuineness of his smile. I took a long drink, wiped my mouth with the back of my hand. "What was he doing here?"

"We have some business I think we can do together. Be great if we can. But I couldn't pass up the chance to get him on our court, even if we can't."

"You go out with him last night?"

Bruce nodded.

"Same spot you took me?" I asked.

"Same spot, different crew. He's always got his guys with him."

"None of the same group we were with?" I asked.

"That was all girls," he said. "No girls last night. Michael just got married."

I didn't hesitate. "There was one guy with us, an older guy. Can't remember his name."

Bruce's expression did not change. "I don't even remember," he said with a wave. "Come on, let's play."

I put the cap on my bottle and rolled it into the corner, beneath the bench where Bruce had sat and watched when Jordan was here. I was not as angry as I had been, but I was ready to play. I was ready to dominate this competition in a way I never had before.

When I turned back Bruce was jogging up the court, grimacing with every step. I felt a pang of regret in my side. "You're hurt," I said. "You don't have to push this."

"Fuck that. I can play."

I watched another minute as he favored one leg, limping badly, cursing under his breath with every step. "Maybe you should rest," I said, my voice no longer angry.

"I don't need rest. I need to wipe this floor with your ass. You play one game with Michael Jordan and suddenly I'm too old and frail for you?"

I took a step toward him. "Bruce, you're the least frail person I've ever met. Right now you don't need to be playing basketball; I think what you need is an MRI."

"Fuck that," he grunted, still jogging, wincing. "Just old legs, that's all. Get 'em warmed up, they'll be ready to go."

I could not bear the sight of Bruce diminished in this way, hobbling about the court, too proud to quit. I ran out in front and blocked his path, forcing him to stop. He all but collapsed into my arms, my sweat mixing with his. "Bruce," I said, holding him up. "You're not that old. You're just hurt. We're going to take a break for two weeks and you're going to rest that thing."

Bruce was out of breath. He looked relieved. "What'll you do?" he asked.

"I need a little time away," I said. "Haven't taken a vacation in years. I'm fried."

Bruce nodded. "You're working too hard. You need balance." My arms were still around him. He pulled me into his chest and gave me a quick hug. "You're a good kid. Go ahead, take Claire someplace, anywhere you want. Use the jet, I'm not going anywhere for a while."

Bruce cared about me. There was no doubt of that. As Ken had said, he did what he felt he had to because that is how he was, but it didn't change the fact that he cared about me. I was as certain of that as I could be. I hugged him back, felt his heart beating rapidly.

"You recharge the batteries," Bruce said. "I'll rest this leg. We'll meet back in this spot two weeks from this minute and I will wipe the floor with your ass."

I made certain he was steady on his feet. "Damn right you will," I said.

He started back toward the elevator, walking now, his limp even more pronounced. When he was gone I went back to my shooting. One after another, the ball felt perfect every time it left my hand. As I shot I wasn't thinking of Bruce anymore, or Percy, or even Claire. Instead, I was thinking about how funny life can be. There are moments when nothing makes sense at all. And then there are moments of total clarity like this one, when you move as though you are gliding on air. And no matter how difficult the shot you try, you simply cannot miss.

IT WAS ALMOST TWO o'clock when I left in a taxi for the Upper West Side.

How the address did not register in my head I cannot imagine, but it did not. My only explanation is that the mind has the capacity to banish information it deems toxic to its own well-being. It is that ability, I believe, that allowed me to glance at the name and address of my father's sixth and final wife and not think a thing of it. There was not a hint of expectation, even as I stepped from the cab. I did not recognize the awning, nor the entrance, nor the lobby, nor the elevator. It was not until the elevator doors opened, when I stepped out onto the sixteenth floor and was instantly overcome by the smell of fresh dill. Then I remembered. Counting squares in the ceiling tiles. Classical music on the stereo. Eating pistachios out of a brown paper bag. The life of a small child. Maybe mine.

Diane was waiting in the doorway of the apartment, the farthest of the four from the elevator. She had a warm smile and large teeth, wearing pearls and a blue dress. "You must be Jonathan," she said kindly. "I'm Diane Gray."

"I used to live here," I said.

"I know."

"It's so familiar."

"I'll give you a moment." She stepped backward and let the door shut gently. She was older than I expected, much older than any of Percy's previous wives, including Mother.

I let my hand trail along the wall all the way to the apartment, where the door was painted blue. I thought it had been red when I was a boy, but I wasn't quite sure; either way, it wasn't the shade of blue it had become.

I tapped gently on the door and Diane pulled it open, smiling broadly, as though she had been here all those years ago and was overjoyed to see me again. "I have wondered if I would ever meet you," she said. "I thought of reaching out to you but thought maybe you wouldn't like that. I want you to know, I am really happy to have you here."

"I'm very glad to meet you too," I said flatly. Of all the places I'd been over these twelve days, this one made me the most uneasy.

Diane stepped backward. "It probably won't look much like you remember, but come in and look around. I'll wait in the living room. Take all the time you want."

I didn't need much time. Most of what I remembered was gone. My bedroom had been transformed into a study: two sturdy oak bookcases overflowing with magazines and papers where my bed used to be. I glanced through the selection of books; nothing unusual, aside from one shelf that contained only those written by my father. I left the room quickly.

The kitchen was entirely different as well. Not a lot of cooking had been done when I was a boy; now it appeared to have been designed for a gourmet chef. The carpeting in the hall had changed, no longer the plush white strands that felt so soft beneath my bare feet. The powder room in the entrance had been remodeled. About the only things that remained appreciably the same were a grandfather clock that stood between my parents' bedroom and my own, and the view, which was sensational but not noteworthy; the Manhattan skyline is by and large the same wherever you view it from. Nothing else stirred my recollection quite like the dill in the hallway. That's the thing about memories sometimes: they smell better than they actually are.

I found Diane on a comfortable-looking sofa in the living room. Her legs were curled up beneath her and she was leaning onto the armrest, balancing a mug of hot tea. The way her body was positioned, she took up almost no space at all. She smiled as I approached and gestured toward a chair. "How do you like it?" she asked.

"It's a lovely apartment," I said. "Totally different from what I remember."

"I'm not surprised. I've been here fifteen years. Changed a lot of it after Percy died." She paused, then said, "I'm delighted you came to see me. It's important that a man knows his father, and it's never too late."

"I'm trying to meet all his wives," I said.

Diane smiled warmly. "I think that is brilliant. Tell me what you've learned."

I leaned back in the chair. "You're a psychiatrist, right?"

"I am. And I knew your father for forty years. And I was married to him on the day he died. So I'm probably the best chance you'll ever have at figuring out anything that might be meaningful to you."

I looked about the room, trying to find anything that appeared the same. "Did you have sessions with my father sitting this way?" I fidgeted. "I mean, you sitting where you are and him where I am?"

She nodded. "We most certainly did."

I closed my eyes. "Then this seems like an appropriate place to end this."

"What are you ending, Jonathan?"

"All of this. I've spent the last twelve days all over the world trying to figure out my father."

"Jonathan," she said in a tone that made me open my eyes. "I feel like you've spent a lot longer than that. And this isn't the end. This is just another step in the journey. I hope it can be a meaningful one, but it will not be the end."

"When will it end?" I asked.

"Probably never."

I shut my eyes again. "I can't decide if I think it's creepy that I'm sitting in the same chair as my father, talking to his shrink."

"I don't think it is," she said. "And I don't think *you* think it is. I know this exercise has been about discovering your father, but the more meaningful discoveries will be those you make about yourself."

I took a deep breath, let it out. Like on the beach in Nevis.

"First and foremost," she said, "you are completely obsessed with your father. It's not just the last two weeks that you have spent in search of Percy, but your whole life. I don't know why you chose now to do something about it, but I am certain this dates back a good deal longer than twelve days. It probably began the last time you were in this apartment. So, not only isn't it *creepy* that you are here, but it is perfect. You might say your whole life has been spent trying to get right where you are now."

I opened my eyes and saw a mirror on the wall. In it, I saw my own reflection when I was eight years old. My father was behind me, teaching me to tie a necktie, measuring the two sides, pulling it tight, right to my throat. His breath smelled of coffee. My mother said: "My, look how handsome my little boy looks!" Percy smiled behind me. I could see him in the mirror.

"Tell me why you went to see all of Percy's wives," Diane said.

"I wanted to know him," I said, my voice thick. "I thought it was the best way."

"It probably was. What did you find?"

I took a deep breath. "My father married my mother because he loved her. She was perfect for him. She was intellectual, spiritual, very political, and beautiful. She had only one flaw: she didn't worship the ground he walked on. Christine did, and that drew him to her. She was attentive and sexy but ultimately shallow, so he grew tired of her and fell in love with Elizabeth, because she might have been as smart as he was, but she was ultimately cold, so he was completely swept away by the gracefulness and beauty of Anne on the stage. The trouble with her was she was too passive. So he found Ciara, who was even more beautiful and probably the strongest and most self-assured woman you could ever meet. But for some reason that didn't work for him either. And then he married you."

Diane took a sip of her tea and balanced the mug again on the armrest of the sofa. "Okay," she said. "So that's what you found. What did you learn?"

"What do you mean? I just told you everything."

She shook her head. "Actually, Jonathan, you told me nothing. You could have read the books they wrote about your father and figured most of that out, would have saved you a lot of time. What matters is not what your father did, but what did it mean?"

I brought both hands to my face. "I don't know," I said. "How am I supposed to know?"

I felt her touch, very gently, on my knee. "I knew your father for most of his adult life. We met at a funeral. That's not much of a setting for anyone, but it was especially tough for him. Your father did not handle death well. I saw him once a week, without fail, the rest of his life. He kept his treatment a secret. He thought it would be perceived as weakness. I didn't agree, but it wasn't my decision to make. I treated him through all his marriages, all his battles, all his victories and defeats."

"Including his son."

"That was his greatest defeat and he knew it. I don't know if that helps at all."

"Should it?"

She smiled. "No one can decide that but you. You seem to want others to give you answers to questions only you understand. I'm telling you that your father died regretting the way he handled his relationship with you. Now, you tell me if that helps."

I breathed in and out. "No," I finally said. "It does not."

She nodded. "Very good."

There was something attractive about Diane the longer you looked at her. Her eyes were clear blue and the lines in her face added character. Say one thing for my father: he had good taste in women. "Can I ask you something?" I said.

"Of course."

"How did you wind up married to my father?"

"Well, he and Ciara weren't together often. He was here, she was there. And I knew it was trouble because he hardly mentioned her at all."

"In therapy?"

"Correct. We had long, involved discussions about his feelings, and often an entire session—a full hour—would pass without her name coming up."

"So he didn't love her?"

Diane shrugged. "With Percy, it wasn't always easy to tell."

"So he left her for you?"

Diane dropped her head to one side. "I wouldn't say that. I was having dinner at Jim McMullen's one night with a friend. Do you remember that place?"

I did, on the East Side. My father loved that restaurant. Mother never went back after they split up.

"Percy came in alone," Diane continued. "It was the first time we saw each other outside the office. He sent a bottle of wine to our table. The next day was our regular session, and he spent the entire hour asking about my life. He kept saying he never imagined me outside the office, but now he was consumed with me. Where did I go? What did I do? He was endlessly curious about the other six days and twenty-three hours of my week."

"What did you think of that?"

"I thought he had decided he was in love with me. All his life, Percy always fell for the woman he thought could give him what he needed right then. I suppose, at the end of his life, that was me."

"What could you give him?"

"Your father was more afraid to die than any person I've ever known. Growing old and infirm was a terrible experience for him. My office was the only place he talked about it. So what I gave him was a little bit of comfort."

"A little bit of shelter from the storm," I said.

Diane smiled. "He always told me Alice loved Bob Dylan."

"She still does."

Diane repositioned herself on the sofa, placed her feet on the floor, smoothed the wrinkles in her long skirt. "Okay," she said. "Enough about me. Back to you. You told me what you found on this journey you've taken. Let's see if we can figure out what it means."

I leaned back in the chair, which seemed as though it should recline but did not. "I guess," I said, "what I learned is that my father wasn't perfect."

"Far from it."

"Does that count?"

"Of course it counts."

"Is it enough?" I asked.

"Enough for what?"

"I don't know," I said. "I feel like there was some answer I've been waiting all my life for, but when I finally tried to find it I realized I didn't even know what the question was."

Diane's entire face changed; she looked ten years younger. "That is *brilliant*!" she said. "In that one sentence you have demonstrated greater self-awareness than I ever heard from Percy."

I dropped my head into my hands. "What are you talking about? I just told you I didn't learn anything."

"Jonathan," she said, "what did you expect to happen? To have a moment where suddenly everything in your life makes sense to you? That's not how it works. You don't get hit by lightning one day and suddenly achieve higher understanding. We are all walking around uncertain and confused."

My head was still in my hands. The image of my father was fading in my mind. I was thinking of Claire.

"Listen," Diane continued, "your father was afraid to die, and if your goal is to live forever you will never be happy. You, meanwhile, seem to be scared to be too much like your father *and* scared that you're not like him enough. So you don't have any chance either."

"So, what do I do?"

"What your father never did. Change the goal."

I lifted my head, looked Diane in the eye. "Change it to what?" I asked.

"Only you can decide that."

From another room, a clock struck three. The chime was achingly familiar, like a musical note. I recognized it immediately as coming from the grandfather clock that still stood in the hallway. The clock was taller than my father. I could recall the joy I took in watching him steer the hands with one finger twice each year, spring and fall. Now, all these years later, I thought if there was one thing of my father's I wouldn't mind keeping it would be that clock. Perhaps I would ask Diane if I might have it someday. Didn't have to be now.

She was looking at her watch. "I don't mean to rush you but I have someone coming shortly. You're welcome to come back anytime if you want to talk some more."

"You still see patients?" I asked.

"I do."

I shuffled my fingers on the edge of the chair. "Can I ask one more question?"

"Of course."

"Do you date anyone?"

"I do not currently," she said in a hopeful tone. "But you never know what the rest of the day may bring."

SONNY WAS WAITING DOWNSTAIRS, just as I instructed. He was standing beside the car, smoking a cigarette, chatting with the door-man as the afternoon traffic roared past. It was starting to rain lightly, ominous clouds rolling in.

"Just sit a minute," I said as I slid into the backseat. "I need to do something."

The rain fell gently on the roof, like the distant beating of tiny drums. I looked up to find the drops had covered the window, streaking my view of the busy street. I put the window down, let the rain fall on my face, took a long, last look at the building.

"All right," I said after a moment. "It's time to go home."

I continued to stare out the window as he pulled away from the curb. The drizzle settled on my cheeks and chin but I didn't put the window back up until we reached the West Side Highway. Then I dried my face with my sleeve, combed my windblown hair with my fingers, and picked my phone up from my lap.

Mother answered quickly. "I'm thrilled you have taken to calling instead of showing up at my door," she said. "While I miss seeing you, I don't gain any weight this way."

"I can have croissants delivered."

"Do me a favor and don't."

"I have a question," I said, "and I don't want you to get aggravated."

"Then don't ask about your father."

I smiled. "One last time. I promise."

"Go ahead."

"Am I like him?"

Mother sighed. "The truth is, Jonathan, you are a little like him and a little not. I know you want a better answer, but there really isn't one."

"No," I said. "That's a good answer."

There was a brief, comfortable silence before she spoke again. I could hear the traffic, the light rain on the roof. "Don't worry so much about your father," Mother finally said. "Are you happy?"

"What?"

"Are you happy?"

I thought for a moment. "Yes, I am."

"Good," she said. "Then go live your life. There isn't any more to it than that."

I dropped the phone in my lap as we passed the George Washington Bridge. In the distance a siren sounded, maybe an ambulance. The traffic was picking up. It was going to take a long time to get home, especially with the rain.

WE WERE ALMOST THERE when the other phone vibrated.

"Quick change of plan," I said to Sonny. "Drive to the beach."

The vibration lasted twenty seconds, then went dead. I didn't take the phone from my pocket, just watched out the window as we made our way to the ocean. The rain had picked up and was coming down hard.

A few blocks from the beach the vibration began again. This time

I took the phone from my pocket and laid it on the seat beside me. Soon it would be summer and this neighborhood would be swollen with New Yorkers. Now it was quiet, not a soul around.

"Over to the dock," I told Sonny, and he drove out past the beach entrance, basketball courts, playground, baseball diamond, skateboard park. At the end of the beach was the entrance to the marina, where Sonny stopped and turned to face me, leaving the engine idling. The windshield wipers were working hard.

The phone vibrated again, on the seat by my leg. I picked it up with the tips of my fingers. "Wait for me here, Sonny," I said, and opened the car door. "I'll be right back."

It was raining pretty hard but it wasn't cold. I glanced around in search of cover but found nothing, so I walked out into the marina. I answered the phone. "Hello."

"Mr. Sweetwater?" There was no doubt of the voice.

"Yes?"

"Mr. Sweetwater, I hope you are having a pleasant day and have had some time to consider our discussion of yesterday. Are you prepared to meet so I can present to you what I have discovered in my investigation?"

The rain was dripping from my hair onto my hand. The clouds obscured the entirety of the horizon. I knew that in the distance the gray met the blue sea, but it wasn't clear where.

"Mr. Sweetwater, are you there?"

The rain was soaking through my suit now. "I'm sorry," I said. "Whom did you say was calling?"

There was a slight pause. "Jonathan, it's Lowell Cranston."

I took one last deep breath. "I'm sorry," I said. "I don't know anyone by that name. I'll ask you to please never call this number again."

The pause was longer this time. "I apologize," he said at last. "I won't disturb you again." I couldn't see him, of course, but his voice sounded like he was smiling.

I let the rain fall on me in silence for a moment. Then I steadied my feet to be sure I wouldn't slip, reached my arm back, and threw the phone as far as I could out into the ocean. I've never had much of an arm but it was a pretty good throw, if I do say so myself.

"When I woke up this morning," I said aloud, "my life was perfect."

I stood and watched the clouds swirl and the waves crash against the dock. I wasn't in any hurry. The air was warm; it was actually rather nice out if you didn't mind the rain. And I didn't. I was so wet already. There comes a point when you just can't get any wetter.

IT WAS FIVE O'CLOCK when Sonny dropped me off at the house.

Claire was on the couch, child on each side of her, arms around them both, watching a television program whose name I don't know. They all turned in unison when I entered.

"Daddy!" Both kids jumped from the couch, came running. They don't always do that anymore. In fact, Phoebe seldom does. I know I need to enjoy it while it lasts.

"Home for dinner," Claire said, walking toward me. "And soaking wet?"

"Got caught in the rain," I said.

"Did something happen to the car?"

"No, it's fine. Everything is fine." I was on my knees, arms around the kids. They were trying to pull away from my watery embrace but I needed another moment.

Claire ruffled my soaking hair. "Oh my, you are *dripping*."

"I'm going up to change," I said as the kids extricated themselves from my arms.

"Want to watch TV?" Drew asked.

"I would love to."

"How about a game of Trouble?" Phoebe asked.

"Sounds excellent."

Her smile melted my heart. "It's just like a Sunday!" she said.

Claire had procured a towel from somewhere and wrapped it around my shoulders. "You're dripping all over the place." Her voice sounded irritated but her face didn't look it.

"I'm going up to change," I said. "Out for dinner tonight? All of us?"

"Let's stay here," she said. "It's too wet outside."

I kissed her lightly on the lips. "Sounds good to me," I said. "I've been outside a lot lately."

I walked up the stairs and turned right one final time. In the guest bedroom I examined the bed, the expensive sheets. There was nothing out of the ordinary. That was the last time I was going check. I'm not going to spend the rest of my life looking for something I don't expect to find.

I'm also not going to spend it looking for something I already have. Life isn't supposed to be perfect. Mine is everything I want it to be and that's more than good enough. I had been leaning this way all along; now the decision was made and I would stand by it forever. In the end, that's what life is about. It really is the sum total of the decisions we make. My father was right. I guess that shouldn't come as a surprise.

We had baked chicken for dinner, with green beans and rice. I opened a bottle of Estancia Pinot Noir and let it breathe while we ate, then I poured Claire and myself each a glass while we played the board game with the kids. When we were finished it was still only seven o'clock. The kids wanted to watch a movie. They settled onto the couch with popcorn and Claire and I went out to the screened-in porch. I brought the bottle of wine, filled our glasses, set the bottle on the floor.

"Pretty night," she said.

It was, despite the rain. The sun hadn't quite set; it lit the sky just enough that the clouds were especially vivid and dramatic. The trees were swaying. A candy wrapper fluttered across the lawn. In the distance I heard a rumble of thunder.

"This is really good," Claire said, holding up her glass. "And I love you very much."

"I love you, too," I said. We clinked our glasses together. "It feels really good to be home."

Claire leaned back in her chair and I in mine, and we delighted in the wine and the wind and all the things our lives had been and everything they might still be. Then she reached out her hand and I took it in mine, and together we stared out into the rain as a flash of lightning brightened the evening sky.

ACKNOWLEDGMENTS

Great thanks, for varying reasons and in no particular order, to Elizabeth Dugan, Dina Siegel, Robert Perlmutter, Robert Boolbol, Diane Johnston, and Betsy Martindale. Also, Andrea Sullivan at Greens Farms Academy, Peter Benedek and Howard Sanders at UTA, Lou Oppenheim and Mark Zimmerman at Headline Media, Richard Koenigsberg at Spielman Koenigsberg & Parker, Katie Steinberg and Tavia Kowalchuk at HarperCollins, and Mark and Jason Bradburn at Morgan Stanley Smith Barney. Special thanks to Kara Edwards, who helped me more than she knows, and Erika Echavarria, for thousands of cosas buenas. And most of all, my literary agent, Jacques de Spoelberch, who has always believed in my writing more than I have, and Kate Nintzel at William Morrow, who continues to understand my writing better than I do.